C000183672

Barry J Calvert is a writer with a unique style. His approach to writing this book was to tell it honestly, warts and all.

He and his wife Marie, have been a part of the swinging scene in Britain for over twenty years, and have experienced just about every facet of recreational sex in this time. Barry has long championed the swinging lifestyle and has appeared on nationwide television on numerous occasions.

Five years ago, Barry and Marie opened 'La Chambre', a club for liberated adults in Sheffield. It now has over ten thousand members.

Swingers 1 is his first book, and it offers a tantalising insight into the mysterious world of 'wife swapping'.

BARRY CALVERT

SWINGERS

1

Matador
9 De Montfort Mews
Leicester LE1 7FW, UK
Tel: (+44) 116 255 9311 / 9312
Email: books@troubador.co.uk
Web: www.troubador.co.uk/matador

ISBN: 978-1905886-647

Typeset in 12pt Bembo by Troubador Publishing Ltd, Leicester, UK
Printed in the UK by The Cromwell Press Ltd, Trowbridge, Wilts, UK

Matador is an imprint of Troubador Publishing Ltd

To Marie, my wife, my lover and my friend

Foreword

I first met Barry and Marie on an engagement at their club La Chambre, in my other guise as a hypnotist, as opposed to my usual appearance on stage as a Grumbleweed. It was with a great deal of trepidation, thirty nine years on stage and not a nerve in sight, yet tonight, absolute fear.

A full audience of Swingers, a bit like Mow Mow terrorists, you know they are about but never meet them in the flesh, but here was I about to try and entertain them. These were those unspoken people who were definitely weird, couples who obviously didn't love each other and openly had sex with strangers.

How wrong could I be? My fears and beliefs were totally unfounded, I had one of the best nights ever on stage.

I met so many wonderful couples that night, some of whom have become good friends, but more importantly, I met Barry and Marie. They had an honesty and openess about them that I found refreshing, I feel honoured to be on their Christmas card list and, in little over a year, we have become close friends.

After being in the company of liberated adults on many

occasions, and after reading this excellent book, I am now of a completely different opinion. These people are not weird or perverse; on the contrary, they have moved on past we mere mortals, shackled by society's unwritten rules of gossip and jealousy, they have dared to spread their wings and fly free.

After digesting this extremely entertaining and enlightening book, dear reader, you will probably feel like me, and realise that our lives can be happy on a different plain, and not just the one we have all been indoctrinated into believing.

I found this book to be one of the most amusing, heart-rendering and informative I have ever had the pleasure to read. Barry tells it just how it happened, in that honest, down-to-earth Yorkshire way of his that typifies the man, and which makes it even more compelling reading.

So whether you are just curious, contemplating swinging, are already a swinger, or just want to have a damn good read, then this book is for you. I guarantee you will savour every page, as I did. Enjoy!

Robin Colvillle
The Grumbleweeds

CHAPTER 1

Beginnings

It was late July 1980. We were sitting in a grotty, little pub in the middle of nowhere, clutching a faded black and white photograph of a couple we were to meet there. We had made contact through a magazine, sorted the meeting arrangements, and now here we were, drinking warm beer out of pewter mugs, somewhere high on the Yorkshire moors and half an hour early.

We were in a state of what can only be described as nervous apprehension, bordering on blind panic. This was because the couple we were meeting were 'swingers', and they had offered to initiate us into the clandestine world of wife-swapping. What had once been a nice, cosy fantasy had developed into a cold, stark reality and neither Marie nor I could quite work out how it had come to this so quickly, and what we were doing in this strange place.

The pub was deserted, except for a couple of locals who eyed us suspiciously. We were probably the only new faces they'd seen in here since it opened, which judging by the decor was around the time of the Vikings. The withered, oak door suddenly creaked open and in walked another local, he nodded to the other two, then stopped dead as he saw us. Our first impression was that we had committed some dreadful sin. Maybe insulted one of their tree gods somehow, or perhaps we were sitting on his bench, the one he'd used every night without fail for the last forty years, and now in he walks and we're sitting on it. That must be a capital offence in these parts.

But just as we had resigned ourselves to being dragged out and burned alive in a giant wicker cage, he regained his composure and shuffled off to the bar to mumble to the landlord and give us sly looks over his shoulder.

Marie whispered that it may be better to wait in the car park, but I was way ahead of her. To hell with the car park, I thought. We should bolt for the door now, jump in the car and head for home, back to the kids, the telly, back to the nine-to-five sex on Saturday night after the match-of-the-day kind of life. That's a safe life, the kind of life normal people live. This is madness, what are we doing here in this weird little pub miles from nowhere, waiting to meet a couple of perverts, who will no doubt want to bonk our brains out as soon as they set eyes on us.

I was suddenly wrenched back to my senses by Marie's strident voice, "Barry!"

"What?" I shouted.

"What do you think?" she continued.

"About what?"

"About the car park, shall we wait in the car park?"

"Yes, yes, the car park. We'll go and wait in the car park," I stammered.

But at that moment, as has happened so often in our lives, fate took control. As the ancient wooden door complained again as it swung open, in walked our couple. At least we think it's them. A quick glance at the faded black and white confirms the family resemblance, but it seems they couldn't come themselves, so they had sent their grandparents instead. They were sixty if they were a day. The photo must have been taken twenty years ago.

Now at this time I was barely thirty years old, and Marie twenty-eight, but even the age thing wouldn't have mattered so much if they hadn't looked as if they had just stepped off the cover of *Farmers' Weekly*. With his greying beard displaying the tell tale brown stain of a committed pipe smoker and the chrome top of a tin of Old Holborn peeping from the breast pocket of his green, padded, body-warmer confirming the fact, he looked every inch the original Farmer Giles. His brown, corduroy trousers and red and green check shirt completed the rustic image. The first thing I noticed about his wife was that she had bright ginger hair, not auburn, not red, but fluorescent ginger hair. It was obviously a desperate attempt to cover the grey, but somewhere along the way she had lost the ability to reason and had emptied the bottle of dye onto her head.

But her hair, bright as it was, still vied for attention with her dress, which featured huge yellow daffodils and a neckline that plunged down almost to her navel to display an enormous pair of talcum-powdered boobs. But the really scary thing was that, apart from a cursory glance, none of the locals took any notice of them, they seemed to fit right in.

They came over to greet us. Marie was smiling through gritted teeth and her expression never changed as she whispered to me under her breath, "Oh Fuck." Pleasantries were exchanged. Farmer Giles got the drinks in and we began to chat, about nothing at first, but slowly and inexorably the conversation came around to sex, and the farmer began to get serious as he told us what they enjoyed. The scenario went something like this. Farmer Giles would hide in the bushes next to a deserted farm track he knew of. His wife would drive by in their Lada estate and feign a breakdown. We would happen to pass a few minutes later and, like good Samaritans, try to get her car started. After failing to start the car, what else is there to do but get her in the back seat and give her a good seeing to, again like good Samaritans. All this time Farmer Giles would be watching and wanking behind the bushes. After a few minutes he would happen along, at which time Marie would invite him into the back seat to see what all the fuss was about.

Now this seemed to be a fantasy they had acted out already, as Farmer Giles was visibly twitching with excitement as he spoke, and Ginger sat spellbound, hanging on his every word, obviously re living delicious back seat memories.

We were much more at ease now and the anxiety we had felt earlier had given way to a kind of bizarre curiosity. These people were like no-one we had ever met before and the truth of it was, I was beginning to fancy Ginger. She had a wicked sense of humour, but it probably had more to do with the huge expanse of bosom that she was flashing at me across the table. But in my heart I knew a session with Ginger on the back seat

4

of her Lada was very unlikely as there was not a snowflake in hell's chance of Marie finding Farmer Giles a turn-on.

This was confirmed a little later, when I got the next round in. Marie ordered a bitter lemon which was a pre-arranged signal that she did not fancy the guy. So we finished the night with more small talk and said our goodbyes.

Now we're in the car going home and I'm feeling peeved, because Ginger was coming on to me all night and I quite liked the idea of trying to get her engine going. So I turned to Marie and said "What was wrong with the guy anyway?"

"Oh, you mean apart from the tobacco-stained beard, the brown teeth, the halitosis breath and the bit of straw sticking out of his ear," she countered.

I shot back, "The guy would have to be a cross between Paul Newman and Robert Redford for you to fancy him. You're too choosy."

"Choosy am I?" she says. "Well at least my criteria for a swap stretches beyond, it has to be female and it has to be breathing."

I toyed briefly with the idea of saying the breathing thing was optional, but thought better of it.

"Shit, I think we've missed the turning. I can't remember coming on this road. Oh great, now we're lost. We spend our whole Saturday night with fucking Davy Crocket and Ginger Rogers' grandmother and now we're lost on the moors. Does life get much better than this?"

I pulled the car over, parked up and stared into the blackness. Marie was first to break the silence with a muffled chuckle, which grew into a loud-infectious laugh. Within seconds we were both in hysterics, tears streaming down our faces and sides aching. We laughed for at least twenty minutes. Every time we thought we'd stifled it, we would look at each other and start again.

All the fears and apprehensions we had kept hidden for the past few weeks now came flooding out in a torrent of laughter. The relief was immense. We have never laughed so much as we did that night on the Yorkshire Moors. Eventually we calmed down and decided to get some fresh air. Leaving the car, we walked about a hundred yards along the narrow heather-flanked road. In the fading light the panoramic view was breathtaking. About a mile to our left, the huge bulk of some un-named mountain rose black and featureless against the clear, night sky. To our right, the land fell away steeply into a valley where a ribbon of road lights followed the valley floor as far as the eye could see.

We made love in the heather, with the pungent smell of peat earth heavy all around us. Afterwards we lay for a while, counting the flickering, yellow lights, where isolated farms clung to the hillside. Except for the faint rush of a river somewhere in the valley bottom, it was totally silent.

The night was warm and Marie had made no attempt to dress after our lovemaking. She now lay on her back, hands cupped behind her head, watching the flashing, red taillights of a jet high in the sky. The moon had given her skin a porcelain appearance. I followed the contours of her body, now outlined vividly against the dark heather, along her thigh, over her stomach and up onto her breasts, only the darkness of her nipples disturbing the whiteness of her skin.

"I think we've had a lucky escape tonight," I said. "We could be stuck in the back of Farmer Giles broken down Lada right now with Ginger, waiting for him to burst out of the bushes." Marie laughed.

"He'd be better calling the AA," she said. "But maybe we'll have more luck next time." The words, next time, had taken me by surprise. After our hapless encounter with the farmer and Ginger, I had expected Marie to have scotched any further attempts at meeting a couple, but perhaps this was not the case after all. I propped myself up on one elbow and looked at her quizzically. She hadn't moved, she still lay on her back, gazing up into the clear, night sky, where the plane's flashing lights were slowly disappearing into the inky blackness, the roar of its engines suddenly echoing around us like far-off thunder.

"So there's going to be a next time?" I asked tentatively.

Marie sat up and slowly pulled on her blouse. "Don't you want to try again?" she asked.

"Do you?" I responded.

"I asked you first," she said disentangling a sprig of heather from her hair.

"Ok," I conceded. "How about we give it one more try and if the next couple we meet are as bad as Farmer Giles and Ginger we'll call it a day, live a monogamous life, and keep swinging as a fantasy?"

"Agreed," Marie answered.

Of course, we couldn't know it then, but the decision we took that warm, July night, high on the Yorkshire Moors, would catapult us into a twenty-year roller coaster ride on the swinging scene. A ride filled with so many memorable moments, some hilarious, some tragic, a ride that would see us cavorting with the landed gentry as well as plumbing the depths with the clandestine hard-core groups. As we walked back to the car, still picking bits of heather from our clothes, I quietly wondered what lay ahead. One thing was certain; life would never be the same again.

CHAPTER 2

Initiation

It had been over a month since our ill-fated meeting with Farmer Giles and Ginger on the North Yorkshire Moors and we were no nearer meeting another couple. We had answered over a dozen adverts from different contact magazines and all we'd had in return were time wasters, and a single guy who had worded his ad as though he was a couple and was now trying to persuade us to have a threesome with him. We were beginning to despair that there were any genuine couples out there. But our rendezvous with the farmer and his wife had taught us something. Even though they had looked like they belonged to a bygone age, their attitude towards sex was light years ahead of our own. The way they had talked so openly and easily about their sexual preferences had been, in retrospect, refreshing. They viewed sex the way most people would view a three-course meal. They would select from a menu and garnish to suit, savouring every morsel before moving onto the next course.

It was an adventure to be enjoyed and shared. Not for them the one-dimensional repetitive meal the vast majority of couples so jealously guard. The more we analyzed our night with them, the more we realised we had been invigorated and intrigued by their unfettered, sexual perspective. We were changing, we knew that, but we were still not sure how or even why.

The phone call that transformed our lives came at seven o'clock on Sunday evening in late August of 1980. It was from a couple we had written to a few days before. They lived in a small village in Lincolnshire and spoke in a relaxed, easy way about receiving our letter and maybe getting together. Marie and I passed the phone between us as if it were red hot, as first Robert, and then Helen, guided us through this first, faltering conversation with experienced ease. After twenty minutes, we hung up, having agreed to go over to Lincolnshire the following Saturday night and stay over. This was breaking our own rules, we hadn't even seen photos of Robert and Helen and here we were spending the night. But something about the quiet, friendly way they spoke and the soft Lincolnshire accent had relaxed us and, although we knew it could turn out to be a serious miscalculation, we felt strangely at ease with the situation. At the very least, this time we would know for sure where our future lay.

The week passed quickly and, with the kids safely ensconced with baby sitters and our overnight bag packed, we set off for the flat, green fields of Lincolnshire feeling the familiar apprehensions rising again. As we drove along the long, straight roads flanked by water-filled dykes, my mind kept going back to the photos of Farmer Giles and Ginger and how much older they were in real life. What if Robert and Helen were the same? True, they had told us on the phone that they were a little older than us, but that could mean anything.

Visions began to flood my mind of hugely obese, seventy-year-old women, wearing tight lycra, and, small, skinny, grey-haired old men, with flat caps and carpet slippers. I looked at Marie for reassurance; she was staring ahead but looked relaxed. She was twenty-eight years old and with the afternoon sun glinting off her blond hair and highlighting her petite features, it was obvious she had lost none of her beauty. She had been just nineteen when we married and the last nine years had been spent making a home and bringing up two daughters. I could not have wished for a better wife or mother and I loved her dearly, as I still do today. But inherent in the love we shared for each other was an isolation, and an overwhelming feeling that we were treading water towards middle age without ever exploring what lay beyond our self-imposed segregation. We were both being driven by the same compelling need to answer our own question, is there anything more?

We knew there was danger in finding the answer, but we were locked into a roller coaster ride, which was already beginning to twist and tumble out of control. The best we could hope for now was to hang on for dear life and hope the answer, if we found it, would not destroy us.

The village where Robert and Helen lived seemed like an island of brownstone houses in an ocean of green and yellow patchwork fields. We pulled up next to the village phone box as Robert had instructed. He said it would be easier to give directions that way. I remember the phone box smelling of pine disinfectant; even the phone book looked like new. I assumed that was normal for this village.

Robert gave me the directions and off we went again. Second turning left, by the post office, down the narrow lane, watch out for the ford at the bottom, only a few inches deep, hardly wets the tyres. Turn right at the old farm gate with the broken hinge and along the single-track lane. Where the honeysuckle climbs the sandstone wall, and there it was, 'Rose Cottage', unoriginal but aptly named, due to the masses of roses covering almost the entire front of the two storey brownstone building. A thin tendril of blue wood smoke spiralled from the chimney. It was an idyllic setting.

But then the images came racing into my mind again to ruin the picturesque scene.

Oh my god! What have we done? And we have agreed to stay the night. Talk about jumping in with both feet!

I almost punched the air with delight when Robert opened the cottage door and walked towards us. He looked normal, about my height, a little leaner but nowhere near thin. He was probably in his mid-forties, with dark hair greying slightly at the sides. He held out his hand, "You made it then," he exclaimed. "No problem, perfect directions," I replied, shaking his hand a little too vigorously. He kissed Marie on the cheek. "Welcome, welcome," he said as he took the overnight bag from her hand. "Come inside," he continued. "There's a bottle of wine cooling in the fridge." Homely is the word that best describes the inside of the cottage. It was small with a low, wood-beamed ceiling, the tiny windows meant there was not much natural light inside, so a couple of ornate table lamps supplied much of the interior light, but this actually added to the cosiness.

A single log hissed and crackled on the small open

fire. "Helen will be down in a minute. Just putting some finishing touches to her face. Please take a seat," said Robert. We sank into the luxurious maroon velvet sofa.

"What a lovely cottage," Marie said. "How long have you lived here?"

"Oh, about three years now" Robert replied. "We're from Grimsby originally. Had a half decent export business there, but once the kids had flown the nest we decided to live a quieter life, have some of what the Americans call quality time, maybe some fun too." He looked at Marie and smiled, she smiled back.

"Oh you mean like cricket or golf?" she said.

"If you can play cricket or golf on a double bed, then yes that's exactly what I mean," Robert replied as he leaned closer to her and poured wine into her glass.

"Well I suppose any game where you get to play with balls has got to be fun," she whispered, slowly sipping her wine and never taking her eyes from his.

My God, she's flirting. My own wife is flirting with another man right in front of me. It unsettled me; I sat there clutching my wine, watching a complete stranger chat up my wife.

Robert was nothing like Farmer Giles, and it was obvious that Marie fancied him. I tried to comfort myself by reasoning that at least Marie would not veto the situation if Helen turned out to be drop-dead, gorgeous. But I had to admit to feeling uneasy at the way Marie was playing up to him. Where was Helen anyway? Perhaps he was one of those single guys who pretended to be married to lure couples in and try to talk them into going for a threesome. If that's the case here, Robert is in for a thick ear.

At that moment I felt strangely alone and vulnerable and could have easily stood up, floored Robert, dragged Marie back out to the car and harangued her all the way home about her unfaithfulness. This was the moment I had feared the most. We had talked about how we would feel when one of us saw the other with someone else. Well, now the moment was here and I was in turmoil. The shock of seeing Marie coming on to another man had caused me to retreat into the past. I had slipped back into our insular lifestyle looking for safety, clinging to the familiar for comfort. As I watched Marie and Robert flirting with each other, I knew I had to make the decision to let go of my insecurities, throw away petty jealousies, swallow my useless anger and embrace the chance to expand our existence. It was a turning point for me, a defining moment. I dug deep, smiled and came out of hiding.

A low, soft voice interrupted my thoughts. "Sorry to keep you waiting.' Helen walked in and sat on the arm of the settee next to me. She was a couple of inches taller than Marie, slender with dark blond hair and hazel eyes. She wore a short black and gold dress that hugged her slim figure and rose a few inches as she sat down, affording me a view of her thighs and the dark band around the top of her stockings. I guessed she was in her early forties, but although she was no longer in the first flush of youth, she exuded the kind of sexual confidence that only older women seem to possess.

The atmosphere was convivial, and as we consumed our third glass of wine the conversation became less stilted and we began to relax, but we were still talking around the edges of things. There had been no sign of anything overtly sexual and I began to wonder if we had somehow misunderstood, perhaps glasses of wine and sexual innuendo was all they had to offer. I felt a mixture of relief and crushing disappointment. Surely we couldn't have read the situation so wrong. We were like children in school, waiting for the teacher to begin class.

Helen stood up and beckoned us all into the kitchen.

"Who's for strawberries and cream?" she said.

"Sounds good to me," I answered, glancing a look at Marie whose eyes widened for a second, which I translated to mean, your guess is as good as mine. The late afternoon sun had cast a warm golden glow over the country kitchen as I sat opposite Helen at the heavy wooden table. Marie sat next to me facing Robert. Helen leaned across the table, twirled a ripe strawberry in a bowl of thick cream and offered it to my mouth.

"You simply must try one of these, Barry," she purred. As I leaned forward to take it from her fingers I felt the point of her shoe between my legs. Helen had placed a spiky high heel up onto my chair and was now steadily working the pointed toe into my groin. Our eyes locked, and I knew without question that there would be far more than wine and conversation on the night's agenda.

The strawberries and cream were swiftly devoured.

"We'll leave the washing up till later," said Robert, as he took Marie by the hand and lead her back into the lounge. I remained frozen at the table.

Helen smiled enticingly, "Shall we follow them?" she asked.

I nodded stupidly, this is it I thought, this is finally it.

I was beginning to panic. "Come on, Barry, stay with this," I told myself. "Don't act like a fool, stay calm."

I was desperately trying to get my head around what was happening. And trying to think of something to say, but my mouth was too dry to form the words. I was also beginning to have serious doubts about my sexual prowess. Helen hooked her finger over the top button of my shirt and slowly pulled me to my feet. I followed her, childlike, out of the kitchen.

We entered the lounge to see Robert and Marie sitting on the sofa, locked in a passionate embrace. Robert's hand was already inside Marie's blouse, and she was making those soft little moaning sounds that I knew so well. I felt no jealousy, no rage, no compulsion to drag my wife away from the clutches of this stranger. The only sensations I felt were the ripples of excitement traveling up and down my spine.

All my preconceptions of how I would react had been blown away; I had gone into a dream-like world, where reality and fantasy began to merge. Helen pushed me gently down into an armchair, then stood in front of me positioning herself between my legs. As I looked up, she took hold of the hem of her dress with both hands and pulled it up over her head, letting it fall to the floor. She stood, hands on hips, staring down at me, with just a hint of a smile on her lips. She had a bigger bust than I had first thought, although it could have been the fact that it was only inches from my face. She slowly lowered herself onto my lap and we began a long, passionate kiss, while all the time she was grinding her body into mine.

I was frantically trying to unhook her bra, but after my fumbling for about three minutes, Helen sat up and with an expert flick of her fingers, her bra slid down onto my knee.

I was thirty years old, but had been transformed into a stuttering, fumbling boy again by this silky, sensual creature. She took total control as she unbuttoned my shirt and then slid my trousers down, after first unfastening my belt. I stood up and stepped out of my clothes. We were soon both naked and Helen pulled me down onto the thick rug in front of the open fire. Our hands began exploring and caressing each other, the surface of my skin seemed to come alive under her fingers.

Something had awoken in me, something deep inside, feelings I had not experienced since the early days with Marie. It was almost as if I was making love for the very first time. I was slowly becoming intoxicated by soft kisses and half whispered words. I let myself be taken on a ride of sensual discovery by this woman rolling beneath me. This was another world, another universe. As we moved inexorably towards the ultimate, our movements gradually quickened and became more frenzied. Helen suddenly let out a long, low cry as she climaxed. I was only seconds behind her, although she was still writhing euphorically for at least a minute after my waves of pleasure had subsided.

I remember a feeling of smugness creeping over me as I watched her lying there with a smile of satisfaction on her face. In truth, she had done all the work. The provocative and sensual way she had guided me through the evening had only served to underline my naivety, a fact re-enforced even more as we watched Robert change positions for the third time, while making love to

Marie. She now lay on the broad back of the sofa with Robert standing between her raised legs, which rested on his shoulders.

He had held off much longer than I had, and as he slowed and quickened his pace, it became obvious that his technique was honed by experience. It was a strange feeling, watching my wife making love to another man while I sat caressing another woman, but it also seemed the most natural thing in the world, and I finally understood all the half-answered questions and never-finished arguments that litter most relationships. Free of the jealously and suspicion, it all became clear at last, and I settled back with Helen's head in my lap to watch Robert and Marie enjoying their own ecstasy. Finally they reached satisfaction. More drinks were dispensed and we all lounged, exhausted, but content in front of the dying fire.

It was a mystifying feeling. We had only known these people for a few hours yet here we were lying naked in their front room. But there in the darkness, the only light from the flickering flames, the only sound an occasional satisfied sigh, the warmth and friendship we all felt was overwhelming. Marie and I had shared more passion and intensity of feeling with two comparative strangers than we had ever experienced with friends we had known for years.

I sat with my back against a chair, Helen's head resting on my thigh. Robert sat with his arm around Marie on the sofa. There was not the slightest hint of embarrassment or awkwardness about the situation. We drank wine and talked and laughed long into the night. Once, just for a moment, we all fell into a contented silence. I looked at Marie, she was smiling. I smiled back, and in the catch of that moment we were hooked, addicted as totally and hopelessly as any heroin addict craving another fix, or alcoholic desperate for another drink.

We had found the answer and now the answer owned us; this was the price we had to pay for knowing, but it was a price we paid willingly. As the grey light of dawn crept through the window, we all crawled off to our beds, and Marie and I had the most erotic sex we had had for years, in a Lincolnshire, rose-covered cottage, which stood on a lane where roses climb the sandstone wall.

CHAPTER 3

Lambs to the Slaughter

The weeks after visiting Robert and Helen were something of a blur for us. We were walking around with our heads in the clouds and a benign smile on our faces. We both felt a kind of superiority to the world at large, not in a pretentious or condescending way, more of a if only everyone could feel as good as this' sort of way. Our benevolence touched every facet of our lives, we were infinitely patient with the children, more forgiving of mistakes made by others. Even being cut up by another car while driving, an action, which invariably brought a response involving two fingers and a four letter word, now only, facilitated an amiable wave and a charitable smile. For we were benevolent, all knowing beings, who had transcended the one-dimensional existence to experience pleasures only a tiny minority of brave souls ever aspired to.

We were on a tremendous high and ready to take on the swinging scene. What we had failed to appreciate in our euphoric but naive fervor was that the swinging scene, or rather the hard-nosed swingers in it, were ready to take us. We were seen as, fresh meat, a term used by hardened swingers to describe new couples who were still susceptible to manipulation. Couples still in the early stages of learning about the scene are easy prey to the experienced, hardened swingers, and in the summer of 1980 when the scene was infinitely smaller that it is today, new couples were a much sought after commodity. Especially if their enthusiasm made them gullible, and in our innocence we were both enthusiastic and extremely gullible. But we were blissfully unaware of the darker side of the scene as we reveled in our new found confidence. My own self-belief had soared and Marie was like a new woman. The realisation that men were lusting after her had given her ego a tremendous boost and she basked in the raw sense of feminine power she had unearthed.

We had been lucky in meeting Robert and Helen for our first experience, they were a genuine couple who had used their knowledge and experience to guide us through the evening with sensitivity and understanding, never once did they take advantage of our innocence. There are many couples like Robert and Helen, good, caring people who nurture new couples and use prudence when initiating them into the scene. But unfortunately there are some couples who take their pleasures any way they can, without worrying about the feelings of others. These people have no concept of mutual satisfaction or respect for the ethics of swinging. They do more damage to the reputation of the scene than all the negative press coverage put together.

One such couple was Kenny and June. They had already rung us half a dozen times since we had answered their letter. They had wanted us to go and see them the very first night they rang and kept pushing over the next week or so until we finally agreed to meet them. There had been no mention of an overnight stay or anything other than our newness to the scene. They appeared preoccupied that we had only met one couple so far, and seemed determined to be the second.

We travelled down to their home in the West Midlands. It was a small, council flat, three floors up a tower block, similar to ones that had sprung up all over Britain in the sixties building boom.

As we stood in the magnolia-painted, inner hallway with its long line of identical front doors, I couldn't help but compare this with the idyllic scene of Rose Cottage which had greeted us just two weeks before. I pressed the doorbell and we were immediately regaled by the chimes of 'Dixie Land' emanating from inside the flat. Marie and I looked at each other and burst into spontaneous laughter.

"Ssshhh," I hissed. "They'll be here any second."

I was biting my lip and nipping the inside of my wrists to keep from laughing. Even as the door opened I could still see Marie's shoulders shaking in silent laughter.

Kenny and June stood before us, grinning like Cheshire cats. They were both about the same height, probably five six or five seven. Neither had made any attempt to dress for the occasion. Kenny wore an old t-shirt and a pair of denim jeans with a rip over one knee. June at least had a sexy, little, brown dress on, but the carpet slippers with the fury bobble didn't quite match up. The peeling wallpaper and threadbare carpets told us they could not be accused of being house proud. This contrasted with Kenny's car, a one year-old Jaguar 4.2, in

British racing green, which he took great pride in pointing out to me on the street below, and June's huge music system, which took up one full wall in their tiny living room. Clearly they were not short of money; they just had different values to most other couples. Their values on sexual satisfaction were no less radical, as we were soon to find out.

We began to feel uneasy as we sat at the cigarette-burned, yellow formica table, drinking tea out of cracked cups. Kenny talked non-stop, hardly pausing for breath, while June stood with her back against the sink, cradling her tea cup in both hands, not saying much, just watching and waiting.

Neither of them could be described as unattractive, but their manner and obvious falseness was lessening their appeal by the minute. We had been there less than half an hour when Kenny suddenly blurted out, "Well time for bed." We looked at our watches, it was only 8:30.

Kenny seeing our confusion tried to clarify, "Well, actually I meant time to go up to the bedroom, eh."

We must have looked shocked, because June interrupted, "At least give them time to finish their drinks Ken." She seemed a little embarrassed by Kenny's haste. We gulped down our tea. No sooner had we finished than Kenny was ushering Marie up the stairs. They were not even half way up before his hand was up her skirt.

Marie gave a shriek of surprise and turned, with a look of alarm on her face. Kenny made a joke about cold hands and Marie forced a smile. I was on the second stair when I felt June's hand pull me back. As I turned she pulled open my shirt, popping the top three buttons.

"Take me here, Barry," June said. "Take me on the stairs."

I glanced up to see Marie and Kenny disappearing into a bedroom. "Shouldn't we go up and join Ken and Marie?" I pleaded.

"No, No, they're fine on their own. I want to fuck you here, on the stairs, now," she panted.

By this time she was tearing at my trousers so hard I thought she would snap the zip.

It was all happening so fast, I couldn't think straight. I was climbing the stairway backwards trying to get to Marie, but June was having none of it. Suddenly my trousers were around my ankles and I fell back onto the stairs. June launched herself onto me smothering me with hard kisses. After a few minutes she slithered down my body and performed oral on me. I was having major problems getting an erection, and June was working like a demon trying to get me hard enough for her to sit on. Eventually she had to compromise. I was only semi erect, but she had done all she could, so it was as good as she was going to get, and she knew it.

Clambering back up my body, she mounted me, and with one hand holding the banister, and the other gripping a stair spindle, she proceeded to ride me like a rodeo cow girl. Every time she lifted and crashed back down, I could feel the base of my spine crunching into the edge of the stair. June's head was thrown back as she continued to bounce vertically up and down on my body. She was shouting out loud, incomprehensible sounds, almost animalistic growls and screeches. She never once looked at me or touched me.

Where was the slow erotic build up, the sensual

seduction that Robert and Helen had shown? It wasn't even lustful. This was just one person using another.

I tensed my body until it was rigid; it was the only way I could keep from being hurt as I lay along the edges of the stairs. June didn't care if I was hurting, she didn't care if I was alive or dead, the only thing she cared about was her own pleasure.

By this time all I wanted was for her to finish so I could get off these damn stairs and find Marie.

Suddenly I heard Marie's voice ring from the bedroom, "Oh yes, oh yes, that's it, come now, come now," but she was faking it. I knew by the tone of her voice, and the words she used. She was trying to get Kenny to come, so it would be over. I felt better hearing Marie's voice, at least she was okay and in some kind of control. It seemed to work as I heard her continue, "Oh yes, baby, that's good, that's so good." Her fake ecstasy had a galvanising effect on June too. As she listened to Marie, she screamed to a shuddering climax, and slumped down onto me, sweating and panting.

I said a silent thank you for Marie's acting ability. After a minute or so June lifted herself off me and, without saying a word, turned and shakily descended the stairs, leaving me alone with my shirt ripped open, my trousers around my ankles, and my senses shredded.

Footsteps on the landing forced my mind back into focus. Kenny trundled past me on the stairs with Marie trailing in his wake. He stopped when he saw my disheveled state, "You look as though you've had a good time," he laughed. Nothing could have been further from the truth. Kenny disappeared into the kitchen. Marie looked bewildered, I knew exactly how she felt.

She put a hand on my shoulder and squeezed. I stood up, fastened the last remaining button on my shirt and pulled up my trousers to find the zip jammed. We walked down the stairs hand in hand.

In the kitchen June was pouring out four cups of coffee, Kenny was already sat at the table. They were laughing and joking with each other, obviously happy with their night's work. In the fifteen minutes it took to drink our coffee, the conversation began to dry up. June kept disappearing into the living room and Kenny lapsed into long, embarrassing silences. It was a glaring attempt to get rid of us. We didn't need telling twice.

The drive home was strained, neither of us wanted to admit that we had been used, and after the euphoria of the last couple of weeks we did not like the feeling of crashing back down to earth.

It took two or three days before we could openly discuss how we felt about our meeting with Kenny and June and what had transpired. Marie, it seems, had suffered much the same fate as I had. As soon as they had entered the bedroom Kenny's hands had been all over her, and foreplay was not on his agenda.

Their general strategy had been divide and rule, relying on speed and our naivety to give them dominance. It had worked; they had used us on the night to extract maximum pleasure for themselves. It was tantamount to rape and our only memory of that night is a sordid one.

How many other new couples had they taken in this way. and how many times had they destroyed what could have been a magical experience? If we had not already been initiated into the scene by Robert and Helen in such a sensitive and erotic way, it is doubtful if we would have pursued a life of swinging. In later years we were to run into Kenny and June again, when we were vastly more experienced and have our revenge, but that's another story. For now, we had fallen from the lofty heights of our benign superiority, had come down with a resounding bump, and felt distinctly inferior.

How could we have allowed ourselves to be manipulated so easily and so completely? In fact, Kenny and June's strategy were standard tactics, tried and tested over many years. These same techniques are sadly still in use today by hardened swingers on newcomers, albeit with much less success due to the fact that to days new swingers are far more knowledgeable.

The huge expansion of the scene in general and its subsequent commercialisation means that new couples are generally more streetwise and aware of the dangers.

But times were simpler twenty years ago, we had no books to read, or television programmes to watch, no websites to log onto, and with our rose coloured glasses firmly on, we were fodder to people like Kenny and June. But we were learning, and learning fast. From now on our enthusiasm would be edged with caution, and our innocence ringed with scepticism. We began to draw up our own rules of engagement and to form contingency plans.

Kenny and June had destroyed our innocence that night, but they had also taught us a valuable lesson, a lesson which we had heeded. From now on, we would be nobody's fresh meat.

CHAPTER 4

Crisis

There was a niggle somewhere in the back of my mind, a kind of itch that wouldn't go away. Marie felt it too. It had begun almost imperceptibly the morning after we had met Kenny and June, and had continued to grow over the six weeks since then to the point where we couldn't ignore it any longer. We had only met one couple since that terrible night in the West Midlands and although the couple was attractive and good company, we had not enjoyed the evening, mainly because we were so much on the defensive we could not relax.

We had turned from naive optimists to hard nosed pessimists and the cracks in our defensive wall had begun to appear. In the beginning, the heady, sexual excitement of it all had carried us along, blocking out the questions that needed to be asked. But now the honeymoon was well and truly over, Kenny and June had seen to that. We now had to face the threat to our relationship that we had chosen to push aside. We had gone into swinging looking for answers, but all we seemed to have found were more questions. There had been tension between us for a couple of weeks. Marie had been snappy and argumentative and I found myself growing increasingly frustrated and angry with the situation. There was a storm coming not just from the rapidly, darkening sky outside but also in our relationship. It would be swift and ferocious and the fear that we may not survive as a couple was a real one.

I took our two young daughters up to bed and read them their usual story. Their plea for a second story fell on deaf ears though. I had decided to front Marie up and bring an end to the tension. As I pulled the curtains in the girls' bedroom, the rain had already begun to beat against the window and the trees at the end of the garden swayed violently from side to side in the gusting wind. Suddenly a flash of lightening illuminated the sky. I kissed the girls goodnight as a clap of thunder rattled the windows.

"Don't worry," I said. "It will blow over soon."

"I'm not worried," said six-year-old Vicky. "I counted the seconds between the lightening and the thunder. It was seven so that means that the storm is seven miles away."

"Clever girl," I said. "So there's nothing to worry about, well, not unless the seconds get down to nothing, which would mean that we're in the middle of it. We'll just have to hope they get longer then," I said.

As I left the girls' room another flash of lightening lit the sky. I was half way down the stairs and had counted to five when the thunder came. The storm was getting closer. Marie stood in the darkened kitchen looking out over the wind, lashed garden.

"Why don't you put the light on?" I asked.

"I don't want it on," she replied.

"Ok, what's going on?" I said. "What's it all about?"

"What's all what about?" she answered.

"Oh, for fuck's sake, Marie," I exploded. "You've been moody for weeks, snappy with the kids, all you seem to want to do is argue or throw silences on me, so don't tell me there's nothing wrong."

Marie turned to me. Even in the darkness I could see the glint of anger in her eyes.

"You want to know what's wrong, do you?" she said. "It's you, you're wrong. You don't give a damn about me or the kids. You're never around when we need you, and when you are here all you do is read the paper or sleep."

"Sleep!" I said. "I'm working my nuts off building a business and trying to keep food on the table and all you can do is have a go at me for being knackered."

Marie pushed past me and stomped into the living room as a flash of lightening flooded the kitchen, followed two seconds later by a clap of thunder.

"Is that it?" I shouted. "Is that why you've made my life a misery — I read the paper and sleep a lot." She was shaking with anger as she struggled to keep her voice below screaming level.

"You don't care what I think, you never have."

"What do you think?" I said. "Please tell me because I really want to know."

She ran past me again and into the kitchen. "Just leave me alone," she shouted as she ran out of the back door and into the garden.

The rain was lashing down and the wind swirled wet leaves and pieces of debris crazily around the garden. She ran to the middle of the lawn and stood there hugging herself, crying. I chased after her, grabbed her by the shoulders and spun her around. Even in the driving rain I could see the tears, the kind of tears only someone in real pain can cry. She was like a wounded animal. I felt as if my world was coming apart. This was the woman I loved and I had somehow brought her to this. It was the worst moment of my life.

Marie looked up at me and sobbed, "You don't love me anymore, I know you don't, I love you so much, but if you don't love me I can't go on." I hugged her to me. We stood on the muddy grass, battered by the storm, tears running down her cheeks, tears running down mine. We just stood there, shivering, beating down our pain and clinging to each other as the storm raged around us, clawing at us, its icy fingers desperately trying to rip us apart, but we held on.

I knew the crisis was over. I loved Marie with all my heart and soul and knowing that she loved me meant we could overcome anything, over and over again I reassured her that I loved her and as we trudged our way back to the house a last, weak lightening flash lit the sky.

Once inside the house, Marie took a towel from the cupboard and wiped away the rain and tears from her face. As she turned to wipe my face, she saw me standing motionless.

"What are you doing?" she asked.

"I'm counting," I answered. As I spoke, a rumble of thunder echoed in the distance. "Fifteen." I kissed Marie and held her close, "Storms over," I whispered. We both changed into dry clothes, I made two coffees and we sat together on the sofa and, for the first time, we talked openly about swinging, about us, about the effect on our relationship and about how we felt. We were being honest with each other at last.

As the night wore on, I asked Marie the question, "Do you want to stop swinging?"

"Yes... no... I don't know," she answered. She sat back on the sofa and looked at the ceiling, thinking hard. "I love the buzz it gives me and we've met some great people."

"And some bad ones," I interrupted.

She laughed. "And some bad ones," she continued. "But sometimes I get scared, I don't really know why. I just start to think that we're doing wrong, and I can't truly love my family or be a good wife if I enjoy sex with other men, and then I feel bad, like I'm a slut or a prostitute. But then I think to myself that I do love my husband, and I would die for my kids, and we're not hurting anybody, and if one of us wanted to run off with someone else, well we could do that anyway.

Hell I could reel off a list of names of women I know who are cheating on their husbands. Some are just out for one night stands, others are having full-blown affairs, so what makes me so bad? At least we're being honest with each other. What do you think?" she asked.

"I think that if you told all those women who are having affairs or one night stands that you were a swinger they would reel back in horror, make the sign of the cross and call you a pervert. We're up against a whole culture here. We've been brought up to believe and conform to that culture."

"Our society indoctrinates us with its own warped morality and when some of us choose to question that morality, we're condemned as weird or perverse. Not only that, but our own subconscious rebels against us because of our indoctrination. It tells us we're bad and have somehow let the side down.

You asked me what I think, I think the only thing we have to worry about is how it affects us and our family and not what everyone else thinks about it. Christ, half the population is out shagging sheep, or having drunken sex with people they meet in nightclubs or pubs, and these are the same hypocrites that leap onto the moral high ground as soon as someone mentions swinging.

If you say to me now you want to stop swinging, we'll stop right now, no questions asked, but let's make sure we stop for the right reasons and not because some frustrated flasher at number 29 says we should."

Marie went upstairs to check on the girls while I made some fresh coffee. It was sometime after midnight. We had talked for more than three hours and I was totally committed to ending our flirtation with swinging if Marie came down and said that that is what she wanted. I stood at the kitchen window, stirring sugar into the cups and watching the last of the black storm clouds disappearing over the horizon. The wind had dropped and the rain had gone, leaving a clean, crisp feel to the evening air. All was calm now; all the murkiness had been washed away.

Marie came into the kitchen. "How are the kids?" I asked.

"Fast asleep," she said taking a sip of her coffee. "I saw that frustrated flasher from number 29 while I was checking the upstairs window," she said smiling.

"Oh yes" I said. "He shouted at me that we should stop swinging as he didn't approve."

"Oh did he now, and what did you tell him?" I asked. Marie took another sip of her coffee.

"I told him to stick his approval up his arse."

CHAPTER 5

Moving Up

Marie had a habit of scratching the end of her nose when pondering something she was not sure of. She was doing it now as she studied a photograph that had arrived with a one-page letter in the morning post. "What's the matter?" I asked."You're not going to believe this," she answered. "It must be a wind up." She handed me the photo and began to read the letter out loud.

> *Dear Couple,*
>
> *Having seen your exquisite ad in the Rendezvous magazine, my wife and I would be delighted if you could attend a Jamboree we will be holding on the 22nd May 1981.*
>
> *The gathering will be couples only and sexual in nature. Dress code is black tie for the gentlemen and short revealing dresses for the ladies. Festivities begin at 9 o 'clock and entertainment will include Vivian the fire, eating transvestite and Dirty Donna 's live eel show Please confirm by post and bring this letter with you on the night. This will be a night of frivolity and decadence. Please be discreet, as shall we. We look*

forward to your favourable reply.
Sincerely yours
    Charles & Georgina Haverington

Please arrive between 7:30 — 8:30pm.
Present this letter as proof of identification at main gate,
Blockley Manor, Chipping Paxthorp.

The photo was no less impressive. It showed a middle-aged couple dressed very conservatively in tweed and tartan standing together on a perfectly manicured lawn, in front of what can only be described as a mansion. Marie was still scratching her nose as she swapped me the letter for the photo. "It looks authentic," I said.

"It can't be," she answered. "I mean just look at them, they could be a lord and lady, or at the very least filthy rich, and who writes a letter like that?"

"Filthy rich lords and ladies probably," I laughed. "Just look at the posh letterhead and the quality of the paper. Someone has gone to an awful lot of trouble just for a wind up. And can you really resist the chance to see Dirty Donna's live eel show?"

Marie stopped scratching her nose, "I suppose if you put it like that."

Almost nine months had passed since our first, tentative steps into the world of swinging. We had learned some hard lessons and travelled many miles. With the kids at home we could not have couples to come to us, so we were always the ones to travel. We had met at least a dozen different couples, two of these couples had become close friends and we had swung together on many occasions. We were no longer the timid, naive couple who had succumbed so easily to Kenny and June. We had not only changed mentally but physically too. For the last three months we had been working out at a local gym and were toned to perfection.

Marie had also bought a second-hand sun bed, which kept us nicely tanned. Swinging had become a way if life, an all-consuming existence, which we pursued with licentious vigour. We were freed from the mistrust and petty jealousies that plague so many relationships, and delighted in discussing in detail what we had done on our swapping sessions, of course none of this would have been possible if we had not been confident of our own relationship. We loved each other and could not have envisaged not being together. Most couples who live monogamous lives find that hard to believe, but then most monogamous couples will eventually end up, either separated, divorced, having affairs or wishing they were. Don't get me wrong, swinging is not a magical cure for a rocky relationship, and it won't solve the problems of a bad marriage, but it will enhance a strong and secure relationship, raising it to new and undreamed of heights of sensuality.

Most swingers will freely admit that the sex they have together after swinging with another couple is intensified to extreme levels of pleasure. This is because they have turned the negatives in their relationships such as jealousy and insecurity, into positives. Losing the insecurities and possessiveness inherent at the beginning of every relationship is a prerequisite to a life of swinging.

These inhibitions can become ingrained over time,

destroying any chance the couple may have of breaking free of these self-made shackles. They cannot see beyond the narrow boundaries they have imposed on themselves. So they continue to live in their one-dimensional world, attacking anything that seems to threaten their safe existence. Swinging is perceived as such a threat, but it is only a threat if you go into it carrying the excess baggage I've already mentioned. In much the same way as you would not go swimming in a heavy coat with a suitcase strapped to your back, do not go into swinging if you cannot rid yourself of suspicion and jealousy. If you do you will surely go under.

We had no such constraints and our lives at that time seemed bright and alive. It was bizarre, there was no question of that, but it was also invigorating, and we loved every minute. We were now fairly experienced in what was then commonly called wife- swapping, but we still had no concept of how deep the scene really ran. We were only scratching the surface, but in our drive for excitement we were already wanting more than straight swapping could give us.

Perhaps this soirée would provide us with the extra dimension we craved. This would be our next step up the ladder. I sat at our kitchen table and wrote a short letter accepting the invitation. As I sealed the envelope, I noticed Marie out of the corner of my eye; she was scratching the end of her nose again.

CHAPTER 6

To the Manor Born

Our lowly Austin Maxi looked decidedly out of place among the other cars queuing outside the main gate at Blockley Manor. I could see a gleaming black Humber Scepture, an S-type Jag, and what looked like a Rolls Royce at the front of the queue. I couldn't make out what was behind us, but as the headlights came half way up our rear window, I concluded it was something big. Marie had bought an expensive new slinky dress for the occasion, and I had hired an evening suit. Standing in front of the mirror before we left home, we had both agreed that we looked highly fuckable. But I had to admit to feeling a little out of my depth when I saw the class of car crunching up the long gravel drive.

We showed our letter of introduction when it was our turn at the gate and we were ushered through. Driving the last few hundred yards to the Manor we were stunned by the sheer size of the place, even the photo had not done it justice. In the massive doorway stood a majestic looking figure in a top hat and tails. His impassive expression never faltered as he watched our humble car drive past. I parked out of the way sandwiched between a Bentley and some sort of foreign-looking sports car with a huge fin on the back. We trod silently over the rich green grass that ringed the front of the huge house, and eventually arrived at the entrance. The commissionaire's eyes flicked expertly over us and for a moment I thought he would call for the dogs to be let loose, but then his lofty brow softened and in a mid baritone voice said, "Would sir and madam please go through into the main hall."

"So far, so good," I whispered to Marie as we walked through the massive entrance hall with its huge chandelier reflecting dazzling light off the gold and silver, ornate wall moldings. We entered the main hall to find a seven-piece orchestra playing soft music to a throng of well-heeled people, who were seemingly oblivious to them. Along the opposite wall lay a long row of silver platters filled with hors d'oeuvres and exotic food.

There were at least a hundred people in the room and the well-bred clamour mixed amicably with the dulcet tones of a Cole Porter melody. There was a general atmosphere of opulence, it was obvious that the cream of the county were gathered here and we felt more than a little nervous about the whole situation.

"Do forgive me; I don't know your names. I'm Charles Haverington."

We were taken by surprise by Charles' friendly manner. I had expected someone aloof and stuffy but he was down-to-earth and seemed very casual, in contrast to the palatial surroundings. I shook his outstretched hand.

"Oh, hi," I stammered. "My name is Barry and this is my wife, Marie."

I pulled the crumpled letter from my pocket, acutely

aware of Marie's disapproval that I had not folded it neatly, "You sent us this invitation."

"Ah yes, the magazine couple, marvellous, so glad you could make it. I must say that ad in the contact magazine thingy certainly had Georgina and myself lusting after you."

"That's very flattering," said Marie. "If there's one thing I love it's a man lusting after me," she laughed.

"Not just me," Charles interrupted. "Georgina took quite a shine to you. Doesn't fancy that many women, says a lot of them are too butch, but you certainly caught her eye." Marie blushed slightly.

"Oh, er, that's very nice of you, thank you," she answered. My mind's eye had already conjured images of Marie making out with another woman. The anticipation was almost tangible.

"Where is Georgina?" I asked doing my best to sound casual.

"Oh the old girl's around somewhere." Charles scoured the room. "There she is, talking to old Windbag Potter, or should I say listening to him. That man could talk the hind legs off a donkey. He does a really funny party piece though; maybe we'll get him to do it later."

Georgina glanced at us and smiled. Her eyes settled on Marie for a second, before Windbag Potter commandeered her attention once more.

"I must say this is quite a gathering, I didn't think there would be so many people," Marie said looking at Charles then at Georgina, and back to Charles.

"Oh, a good half of them are just here for the entertainment. We'll get down to the real players after midnight. You will be staying for that won't you?" he implored.

"We'll be staying," we answered in unison. Charles laughed and took hold of Marie's hand.

"Then tonight you shall play as you have never played before." He bent down, kissed her hand, and then grabbed the arm of a passing white coated waiter. "Emille, some champagne for my guests, and Emille, I want you to take special care of Barry and Marie. See that they have all the food and drink they want."

"Of course, sir," said Emile.

"I have to mingle now, but Georgina and I will see you both later when we'll have more time to get to know each other." Charles then disappeared into the crowd. We drank our champagne and no sooner had we drained our glasses than Emile was there with two more.

"The magazine couple," said Marie indignantly. "I think that's how posh people talk."

"Seems like a nice enough bloke though," I answered.

"Yes, he's ok," Marie said matter of factly. She was playing it cool, but I knew she had been intrigued when Charles had mentioned Georgina's liking for her.

I decided to play it cool too, "I wonder what happens after midnight?" I asked.

Marie looked up at me and began scratching the end of her nose. "Well I doubt very much it has anything to do with turning into a pumpkin."

Emile was never far away as the evening progressed, and by the time Vivian, the fire-eating transvestite took centre stage we were beginning to feel more confident in our opulent surroundings.

Vivian stood about six feet three in his high heels and was dressed in a red PVC cat-suit. His act consisted of blowing huge plumes of flames into the air, whilst dancing erotically around the floor. The trouble was, once you had seen him blow his flame and dance his dance for the seventh time it got boring and people began to drift away. So, in a desperate attempt to keep his audience, Vivian began to blow larger and larger flames and take massive mouthfuls of fuel. It was bound to end in disaster as finally he hiccupped, swallowed half the fuel and coughed out the other half, sending a sheet of flame into the crowd. Luckily no one was seriously hurt, just a few singed wigs and blackened faces, but I think it was safe to say Vivian had now lost his audience, so he reluctantly retired to the bathroom, where his retching could be heard for a good twenty minutes.

With Emile in our slip-stream and the warming effects of the champagne beginning to work, we began to move among the distinguished throng with confident ease. They were a mixture of wealthy industrialists and country aristocracy and, far from being overawed, I found myself bolstered by a feeling of working-class superiority. And, in the best male chauvinist traditions, I really fancied getting one of these posh birds bent over and showing her how a working-class lad from the back streets of Sheffield does it.

Twenty years on and with the benefit of hindsight, I was trying to prove a point, mainly to myself I suppose. I resented feeling inferior to these people. My working class upbringing had bred into me a deep hatred of the class system, and yet here I was mixing with the enemy. Not only that, but finding them decent, friendly and fun to be with. The inner conflict had triggered an instinctive defence mechanism, meaning my need to screw one of their women was not so much sexual as tribal.

I still had a lot to learn, and, although I had vastly improved my love-making technique over the last few months I still believed penetrative sex to be the ultimate in sexual enjoyment. But as the night wore on I became less and less defensive and the endless glasses of champagne had given a rose coloured hue to our view on life. Emile was still following us and looked crestfallen when we refused his offer of more bubbly.

Dirty Donna's live eel show was next on the agenda and eagerly awaited by all. We were fascinated by just what Dirty Donna was going to do with the eels. In the event it turned into another fiasco, as one of the eels wriggled from her grasp and slithered snake-like along the floor and through the feet of the audience. Women screamed and men laughed as Donna repeatedly attempted to pick up the creature, only for it to slip from her grasp time after time. Eventually she made a desperate, last lunge for the eel, skidded on the wet floor, fell and dislocated a finger. The age-old shout of "Is there a doctor in the house?" brought at least four men and a woman forward. The eel was eventually captured in an ice bucket and returned safely to its tank. By now the whole room was in uproar. People were falling about laughing, while a couple of the women were crying and being consoled by their partners.

Through the general melee I could see Charles button-holing Windbag Potter, and beyond him Georgina had her arm around a grimacing Dirty Donna, while two of the doctors improvised a make shift sling.

The sound of a spoon on a champagne glass brought everyone to order. Charles stood on a chair in the centre of the room and made an announcement. "Ladies and Gentlemen, due to the unfortunate accident that has befallen Dirty Donna, I'm afraid that her live eel show cannot now take place." A hum of disappointment rumbled through the crowd. "I must also apologise to those of you who were incinerated by Vivian earlier." This brought a murmur of amusement.

"But you will be pleased to know that there will be no lasting damage to Vivian, or indeed his audience, but the doctor has asked him not to smoke for the remainder of the night due to the risk of an explosion." A pall of laughter now engulfed the room. I don't know what Charles did for a living, nor indeed if he did anything at all, but he certainly had a gift for public speaking. The assembled throng were now firmly in his pocket. He continued, "But fear not my esteemed friends and colleagues, for we have one amongst us who will entertain and delight us with his now-legendary rendition of the mad scientist. Ladies and gentlemen, I give you Reginald Livingstone Bartholomew Potter."

A boozy cheer echoed round the great hall as windbag Potter stepped forward. He was a large portly man in his late fifties with receding hair, a red complexion, and huge jowls that wobbled when he spoke. An expectant hush descended on the room as Windbag began his preparation.

First he dipped his fingers in a glass of champagne and ran them through what was left of his hair, spiking it up on top and pulling it out from the sides. Next he took off his coat and unbuttoned his shirt almost half way down, then dragged his dickibow round to the side of his neck. Slowly his big, red, bloodhound face took on a crazed look, his eyes bulged, jaw jutted and his nostrils flared like a Grand National winner. The transformation was complete, he was the mad scientist.

Suddenly he grabbed a bread stick from the buffet table to use as a blackboard pointer and in a mock German accent launched into action. "Now here ve see zee molecules arranged in zee random pattern," he pointed to a tray of vol-au-vents with his stick, "Vale over here, zee molecules are in zee pattern of zee open vagina." He bounded over to a tray of salmon paste sandwiches, arms flaying and breadstick swishing, "Ziss is goot, yah." He then picked one of the sandwiches up and sniffed it. A huge grin spread over his face, "Ziss is very goot." He then ate it. "Mien got zat vos even better." Then he impaled a sausage roll with his bread stick pushing a bit of sausage out of the end. "Now vee see vot happens ven zee erect penis enters zee orifice." As he spoke the bit of sausage fell out of the roll. "Ooops zat vas zee wrong orifice." I had to admit this was funny, and Windbag was now in full flow.

His performance involved expending vast amounts of energy as he bounced and leapt around the room. He was not a young man but he was revelling in his moment of glory, and the audience loved him.

Most agreed that this was his finest performance ever of the mad scientist. The grand finale came as he began rubbing the breadstick. "Vee see how zee molecules remain erect ven I do this, ahh you like to touch the molecule," he said to a laughing middle aged lady who was standing close by. To his surprise she took hold of the breadstick and broke off the end. "Ahh vot have you done, zee pain, zee pain." By now he was leaping around the room seemingly in some sort of spasm. "Help, help. Zee Russians are at zee Reichstag, man zee barricades. I voz only following orders. Vot is happening to me? Help, help. Take me to Argentina. Do you know a goot plastic surgeon?"

By now the entire room was in uproar and Windbag was going for an Oscar. "Vait, vait, its too late, all is lost." Windbag stood still for a moment. "Ziss is the end, goot by my friends, and vot ever you do don't eat zee breadsticks." With that Windbag gave a last convulsive jerk and dropped stone like onto a chair.

We clapped and cheered with everyone else. His portrayal had been masterful and the room rang with laughter, which eventually turned into a vibrant hum. Windbag Potter was still being congratulated by a succession of adoring fans as Emile reappeared at our side, and his face lit up when we accepted a drink from his tray. My watch read eleven-thirty and people were beginning to leave. By five minutes to twelve, well over half the crowd, including Windbag, had boozily said their goodbyes and departed.

When the exodus was over around forty couples remained and a polite buzz of conversation brought a more sober atmosphere to the party. I noticed one or two of the couples being ushered into another room by Georgina. We continued the polite chitchat, all the time watching a steady trickle of people leaving the room.

The conversation ended abruptly as Charles entered the room. "Can I have your attention, ladies and gentlemen? Now that the non-players have left, the real party can begin. If you would all follow me. please."

We joined the migration and followed Charles into a large ante room off the main hall. In the centre of the room, strapped to a huge, oval bed was a naked woman, her arms and legs splayed out like a skydiver. "Please feel free to use her anyway you wish," said Charles.

Georgina then took over the tour. "If you would care to follow me."

We all trooped into another, adjoining room where a naked man, strapped to a makeshift whipping post, was being lashed by a rubber clad, dominant-looking woman. On the other side of the room were two massage tables, beside which stood a male and a female masseur, both dressed in shiny, black PVC.

Georgina pointed to the man tied to the post. "If anyone would like to learn the art of chastisement, then I am sure Mistress Melissa will be only too pleased to teach you."

The dominant woman ran the whip through her fingers and nodded. "And these two give the most erotic massage. I really do urge you to try them. And now my friends, let the games begin."

Within seconds the crowd had dispersed; some made their way back the way we had come; some began taking off their clothes where they stood; others just sort of milled around. I kept expecting Emile to appear at any moment, but we had seen no sign of any of the waiters since the mass exodus at twelve o'clock.

We almost felt abandoned by his absence, but to us, this was like two kids let loose in the proverbial sweet shop. Everywhere we looked something was happening.

If this was the next step up the ladder, then we were ready to climb.

Marie was wide eyed with anticipation. "Where would you like to start?" I asked.

"Wow!" she answered, "We're spoilt for choice."

"Then lets start at the beginning," I suggested.

We made our way back into the first room where the naked woman was strapped to the bed. Now, at that time we thought we were unshockable, but the sight that met us as we entered the room startled us. Charles had said that she could be used, and she was. Two naked women were sucking her nipples, whilst another straddled her face, a naked man was pounding in and out of her whilst at least three others were running their hands over what spare skin they could find. Whenever the woman who was sat on her face allowed it, the prone female shrieked with pleasure. We watched open-mouthed as one person after another climbed on her resulting, in a tangle of limbs. Someone then produced a huge rubber dildo which was greased and slid into a spare orifice, while a semi-naked woman lapped at her pussy. It was incredible, like nothing we had seen before. We watched in amazement as a procession of men and women used the helpless female. There was no doubt she was loving every second. I don't think I have ever heard so many ecstatic sounds coming from one person.

Marie gripped my hand, "God this is turning me on," she said.

She was right. This was pure, unadulterated lust. It was perverse and erotic, pornographic and decadent, and we were buzzing.

"Let's see what's happening at the whipping session,"

said Marie, as she dragged me into the other room.

The naked man was being whipped by a succession of willing ladies. His back and backside was striped and reddened, but he barely made a sound as woman after woman flogged him.

Then someone handed the whip to Marie, "Would you like a go?" they said. Marie looked at me as though for approval.

I nodded. "Go for it," I said. She took the whip, stood back for a moment and let fly. It landed square on the man's back. He flinched, but still made no sound. She ran the leather thong through her hand and licked her lips. Again the crack of the whip, this time leaving a purple stripe on his backside and forcing a yell.

Marie was now getting into her stride. She seemed captivated by the domination aspect. I had never seen this side of her. Her cheeks were flushed and she was panting, but not from exertion, more from the exhilaration she felt from dominating a man sexually. She would tell me later that she never knew this side of her existed until the moment she felt the whip in her hand. This was a new and exiting development in her own personal expansion. I had always known she had a strong side to her character but a dominatrix, never! But it was clear that she had found a niche, and I was astounded by the look of satisfaction on her face as she reluctantly handed the whip to someone else.

This was why we were here, why we were involved in the swinging scene, to expand our existence, to find out who we were, and explore what we could become. This was also another of those defining moments. It would have been easy to panic and run when presented with a side of yourself that shocks you and was hitherto unseen. But we had learned not to run and hide from life but to embrace and nourish it. Marie had climbed the next rung of her own personal ladder and was ecstatic.

She ran to me, threw her arms around my neck and kissed me passionately. "I love it," she shouted.

"I love it." Charles and Georgina had been looking on while Marie had been enthusiastically whipping the poor guy, and now they came over.

Georgina kissed Marie full on the lips, "Quite a turn on, beating a slave, don't you think?" purred Georgina.

Marie looked flustered, this was another first for her, we had toyed and fantasized with the idea of Marie making it with another woman, but the timing had been wrong or the opportunity had not arisen. Male homosexuality is generally frowned upon in the scene, and I have never felt the slightest inclination to have sex with another man. I'm making no moral judgment; I'm just stating my own preference. But a large percentage of women in the swinging scene are bisexual and this is actively encouraged by both sexes. Dual standards it may be, but the old morality that prevailed in the seventies and eighties is just as strong today, perhaps even more so. Some things never change.

Georgina dragged her eyes away from Marie and studied me, a sudden realisation hit her. "Ah, the magazine couple. Barry and Marie, isn't it, sorry I haven't had the chance to talk to you before now, what with that awful Vivian person trying to burn the place down, and the thing with the eel."

"It's ok," I answered. "At least old Windbag came through."

"Ah yes, Reggie Potter, I think he planned the whole thing just so he could play the mad scientist, again," she laughed. As we spoke I was conscious of her closeness, the sweetness of her breath and the aroma of her expensive perfume. She wasn't classically attractive and her figure, although slim, would have benefited from a few sessions with us in the gym. But her supreme confidence overshadowed her less-than-perfect body and gave her an attractiveness all of its own, and I still had this primitive ethnic urge to give it to the posh bird, good and hard.

"Yes. One way or another it's been a very stressful night," Charles said, "but I think a nice, relaxing massage may just loosen us up. What do you think Georgi?"

Georgina turned towards me, "Would you like to experience the ultimate massage, Barry," she whispered. I noticed how she had lingered on the word ultimate. "Sounds great. lead me to the bench," I answered confidently. I was determined that I would not be overawed by whatever Georgina had in store for me. I was not the shy, stumbling first-timer anymore, and if Georgina wanted to tease and taunt the working-class bloke from the magazine she would find I was ahead of the game.

She lead me over to the massage tables which had been pushed together to make a double bed arrangement. "Take off your clothes," said Georgina, as she began to slip out of her dress. Charles and Marie were looking on smiling. If Georgina's plan was to embarrass me by making me strip in a room full of people, she had failed. I had done this dozens of times in front of other couples, and all the gym work had paid off. I had a good, muscular toned body, so shyness was the last thing on my mind as I stepped out of my shorts and stood naked, facing Georgina.

She stood for a second, giving me the once over. She was impressed. I had seen that look before, on the faces of different women, who usually expected me to resemble their own partners, with their beer bellies and ultra-white flesh. Marie and I knew there had to be a good reason why we sweated buckets in the gym bench-pressing, peck-decking, scrunching and tread-milling, and why we spent long, boring hours cooking, until golden brown, on the sun bed. The reason was moments like this when the person in front of you stands wide-eyed in admiration and approval. It's a good feeling.

Eventually she pulled her gaze back up to my eyes.

"Climb aboard," she whispered, as she pulled herself on to one of the beds. Soon we lay side by side on our backs; Georgina took hold of my hand and said, "We're ready." Within seconds, the male and female masseurs stepped forward and poured a full bottle of warm baby oil over each of us. The PVC-clad blonde female began to rub the oil over my body whilst the male masseur did the same to Georgina. We still held hands, fingers interlocked, as the warm oil was spread over our skin by the skilled hands of the two masseurs. The slow, rhythmic motion was relaxing and, at the same time, incredibly sensual. The two masseurs were working in unison, as one went higher so did the other, when my masseur kneaded my chest Georgina was having her breasts massaged, and when Georgina's masseur worked on her groin area mine gently caressed my genitals. I rolled my head towards Georgina. She had her eyes closed and was groaning softly. This was intoxicating. I had forgotten about the other people in the room. No one else seemed to matter, as I began to lose myself in a soft, cloud-like waking dream. We were still holding hands, sharing this sublime experience.

Slowly, almost instinctively we turned towards each other and began to kiss, long, slow, luxurious, oily kisses. Then just as slowly and imperceptibly, our hands began to explore each other, our finger tips skimming the surface of the skin, following the creases and contours of our bodies to dark, damp, carnal places. We were making love now, slow, soft, slippery love. The masseurs were still kneading and rubbing our bodies, still stroking and caressing as we lay locked together, grinding inexorably to a prolonged, earth shuddering climax.

I did not think it possible, but we went higher, into another realm of pleasure. This transcended any level of eroticism I had experienced in couple to couple swapping. It wasn't hard, or lustful, or tribal. I had ceased to be aware of my previous desire to take one of the rich men's women and screw her hard. I had lost the need to defend my origins, like a blind man seeing the light for the first time. I realised that sexual ecstasy is not always about stamina and endurance. It sometimes transcends the physical body and resides in the mind, or the soul, or that part of us that is left when the body reaches its limits and we have to look to the spiritual for direction.

To reach this level of euphoria is more luck than judgment. It's like finding the centre of a maze. You may come across it once or twice but most of the time it can't be found, no matter how hard you try. In twenty years, I've only been to that level of sexual bliss on six occasions and don't forget I've been out there looking for it on the front line. So don't beat yourself up if you haven't experienced it yet. It's enough to know that it exists and that, like the centre of the maze, it can be found.

I certainly found it that night. I remember thinking that it doesn't get any better than this. I remember looking around at the profusion of naked writhing bodies and hearing another crack of the whip as a rubber clad mistress lashed the tethered slave. I remember the smell of scented oil mixed with perfume and perspiration, and I remember the excited realisation on Marie's face when she discovered she had a penchant for domination. I remember the ecstatic screaming of a woman who was being turned inside out by half a dozen people. I remember watching Charles and Marie making love on a chair, while watching the slave's back turn crimson red and I remember jerking and convulsing uncontrollably to a mutual climax with Georgina on an oil covered, padded bench as two masseurs held on to us to keep us from falling off.

I remember so many things from that night, not least when Marie and I followed Charles and Georgina into a room covered from floor to ceiling in red crushed velvet. Charles closed the door when we were all inside, then turned to me and said, "Barry, most men would give their right arm to witness what we are about to see."

The room was small, maybe ten by ten with a single red light suspended from the ceiling, giving a dull, ethereal glow. Spread around the room were half a dozen large, red velvet cushions.

Charles continued, "Sit down my friend and enter heaven." I sat on the nearest cushion. Charles sat on the other side of the room facing me. Marie stood in the centre with Georgina. She looked slightly bemused, but she knew what was about to happen, and I knew she wanted it to happen, craved it. Georgina moved behind her and ran her hand up Marie's hips to her breasts. For a second Marie froze, but as Georgina gently kissed her neck, she began to respond. Turning to face Georgina they began a long, slow, passionate kiss. Marie's hands skipped over Georgina's body, expertly maneuvering into places not considered by most men as pleasurable to a woman, but which brought gasps of delight from Georgina.

The image of them is as clear to me today as it was then. I watched in awe as they licked each other, necks, breasts, belly, vagina, everywhere, slow and serene with eyes closed like untamed cats in a red velvet jungle.

No man could have matched the sensitivity of their touch. Marie describes it as butterfly fingers, and no man could master the delicate ambience of the moment. Here were two women, unashamedly surrendering to the hunger within them. As I sat there, spellbound, listening to Marie panting in sharp bursts, and Georgina moaning or purring, depending on what Marie was doing to her at the time,

I realised that this was the most erotic thing I had ever seen. I had never considered that just watching could be so much better than doing. I was on the learning curve again. Perhaps it's not all about penetration after all. The working class bloke was being forced to face the fact that his beliefs were flawed, and the doctrine to which he had aspired and had perfected to a degree was, at best, outdated and, at worst, offensive.

I was on a journey of discovery, and it hit me like a hammer to suddenly find that the macho, stud image I was trying to cultivate had been so totally eclipsed by the soft, sensitive, spiritual side of sexual enjoyment. I believed then, as I do now, that many men will not admit to the truth of that statement because they fear the threat to their manhood that it implies. The realisation that penetrative sex is not the ultimate pleasure shakes the male chauvinist to the core, but I gave little thought to the ramifications of my discovery as I watched Marie and Georgina kiss, fondle, and tongue each other.

I was struggling to find the words to describe what I was seeing. It was soft, smooth, serene and pure. It was erotic, seductive, intoxicating and forbidden. It was all those things and more, yet still I could not fully explain the sensations rampaging through my body. The two women were now locked together, entwined in a fusion of female sexuality.

They had moved to a part of themselves that dealt only in movement and rhythm. It was reminiscent of some mystical tribal dance, which had transported them and us to shadowy, far away places, where the only thing that mattered was being there, in that red velvet room at that time, nothing before or after had any meaning, only the movement.

I could see Charles on the other side of the room. He was transfixed, hypnotised by the beauty of it all. As the great, spiral dance finally slowed and came to an end, the two women lay drained and spent, wet with their own sweat and juices. They twitched and shook, as they steadily descended into normality, bringing Charles and I with them in their wake.

Nothing could have prepared us for that night; no book could have told us just how we would feel; no person could have explained the emotion we would experience. We grew that night. We vastly expanded our knowledge and understanding of sexuality, not just the physical doing of it, but the perception of it. It was like looking at an abstract painting and suddenly understanding what the artist is saying, instead of just enjoying the shapes and colours. I realise that is probably a poor analogy but it is the best I can do. It's one of those things when you really have to be there.

The party carried on until dawn. Marie made love with a doctor of some kind, while I finished off the night having a pretty decent session with a red-head on the big, oval bed. It took us almost a week to recover from that party. Marie's legs wobbled for days and all I seemed to do was sleep.

We have met Charles and Georgina on many occasions over the years. Every time they call us they will jokingly say, "Is that the magazine couple?" And I often remind Charles of what he said to me on that night. I can still hear his cultured tones,

"Barry, most men would give their right arm to witness what you are about to see."

I have said these same words to other men many times, over the years, and have never met anyone who has seen what we saw and disagreed.

CHAPTER 7

Wild Times

Our night at Blockley Manor had been an exquisite experience, but just as importantly, it had been an education. We had learned more in one night than all of the previous year, and I think it would be safe to say, for a time after Blockley Manor, we ran wild and threw ourselves headlong into the lifestyle. Charles and Georgina had opened our eyes to a whole new dimension and taken us to new levels of excitement and pleasure, and our thirst for more of the same led us to rush in where others feared to tread.

One of these rushes led to us meeting a very attractive but strange couple from the Norfolk Broads. We went to a barge they told us they lived on, but it was way too small and very poorly equipped to be a home. And our suspicions were confirmed when Marie found a metal plaque riveted to the inside of a cupboard door saying the boat belonged to a Lowestoft company and was available for hire. We weren't unduly concerned, if they wanted to keep their home address secret that was their business. After all we were there to screw them not rob them, although we began to wonder what kind of people we had landed ourselves with when they asked us very politely if we would mind filling out a questionnaire before we got down to business.

They said it would help save time and make things run smoother if we all knew each other's likes and dislikes before we began. If we had been asked to do this by someone we had just met, a year previously, we would have run a mile, and a year later we would have told the couple where to stick their questionnaire. But as I say, at that time we were game for anything and hell bent on fun, so if it meant playing twenty questions and making it with this good-looking couple so be it. If my memory serves me right the questions read like this:

1. Age
2. Sex
3. Favourite position?
4. Most sensual part of your body?
5. Do you kiss with your mouth open?
6. Are you bi-sexual?
7. Would you consider anal sex?
8. Are you a long stayer?
9. Are you into bondage?
10. Do you like group sex?

Marie answered her questions like a schoolgirl sitting an exam studying each one before carefully writing down the answer, but I couldn't help playing the naughty school boy and decided to have some fun with mine. My completed form read:

1. Age. of Aquarius.

2. Sex. Yes Please.
3. Favourite Position? Centre forward.
4. Most sensual part of your body?
   Big toe – left foot.
5. Do you kiss with your mouth open? Only after
   eating garlic.
6. Are you bisexual? Only with straight people.
7. Would you consider anal sex? Consider it done.
8. Are you a long stayer? I never outstay
   my welcome.
9. Are you into bondage? Only when I can 't get
   out of it.
10. Do you like group sex? Only when I'm alone.

Of course, when we all swapped our bits of paper I was admonished for not playing the game. Marie gave me a look that said stop fooling around, so I dutifully filled out another questionnaire and we proceeded to have a very enjoyable night, making the boat rock, even if it was a bit like shagging by numbers.

Around that time we also discovered the delights of flash cruising. This entails driving along the motorway in the early hours when there is very little traffic (we would do it on our way back from a swinging session, usually around 2 or 3 in the morning) and pulling up along side a lorry. I would then turn on the interior light, honk the horn to get the driver's attention and Marie would strip off and play with herself and generally put on a show for the lucky lorry driver. The knights of the road usually appreciated the impromptu shows so much they would blast their sirens like a train driver blowing off steam. We once went down a fleet of about seven or eight wagons one night, giving each one a minute or so of Marie playing with a dildo. By the time we got to the last one they were all blasting away with their horns. It must have sounded like a cavalcade to the people living close to the motorway.

Flash cruising was popular with lots of swingers around that time and many would drive out to the motorway in the early hours just to have fun looking for slow-moving lorries. Some couples used to take flash cruising a step further by opening the sunroof and letting the women stand up. This could only be done at low speeds because of the wind factor. We tried it a few times, after we had bought an Austin Princess, which, was the first car I ever owned which had a sunroof.

One of the couples we were seeing at that time was Gavin and Lindsey from Scotland and, being typical of swingers from north of the Border, would try anything once. We told them that we had flash cruised with the sunroof open and Marie had flashed her boobs at an overjoyed lorry driver and they were keen to give it a try. The next time we saw them was about four weeks later at a house party in Newcastle, they were talking to another couple but we noticed straight away that Lindsey was covered in tiny red marks and bruises. When Gavin saw us, he came over.

"Remind me never to trust the word of a Sassenach," he said jokingly."

"What have we done wrong?" I enquired.

"Well, you know when you told us about flash cruising, with Marie stood up through the sunroof?"

"Yes," I answered.

"Well we tried, it about a week ago we were coming

back along the motorway in the wee small hours and we spied a slow-moving lorry in the distance, so I speeds up to him and Lindsey jumps up through the sunroof with her tits out and guess what happened?"

"What?" I said.

"We were sprayed with half a tonne of gravel" said Gavin. "It was a gritting lorry." Marie and I both burst out laughing."

"It's ok for you two" said Gavin. "Just look at Lindsey. She looks like she has the measles. We'll get fuck all tonight with her looking like a pin cushion. But do you know the worst of it?" continued Gavin.

"There's more?" I said wiping the tears of laughter from my eyes.

"Och aye," said Gavin. "That damn gravel gets everywhere. I'm still picking bits out of the upholstery and it's ruined the paintwork." A true Scotsman was our Gavin.

Looking back, this was a chaotic and dangerous time for us. We were criss-crossing the country every weekend in our quest for adventure and, to be brutally honest, we were less than choosy. We were like two kids on a toboggan, loving the ride but having no idea how or where we were going to stop.

We visited an odd couple who lived in an old farmhouse high in the peak district. The house itself was blackened with age and in a bad state of disrepair. Inside it was dark and dismal, with old, dusty paintings adorning the walls. Above the iron fireplace hung the head of a stag mounted on a wooden shield. I tried to lighten the mood by saying that the stag must have been really moving to have embedded itself so deep. But my attempt at humour was met with a stony silence. Their conversation resembled something out of an old B movie and the clothes they wore looked to be a mix-and-match from a jumble sale. At one point in the evening Len, or at least that is what he called himself, was showing Marie a painting that hung on the back wall and had said it had belonged to their father. As soon as she could, she came over to me and whispered, "These two are brother and sister," then proceeded to tell me of Len's slip of the tongue. The more we looked at them the more we could see the family resemblance.

"What shall we do?" I asked when they had both left to make a fresh pot of tea.

Marie just shrugged and said, "Keep it in the family I suppose."

When we eventually got down to business, I found I had a wildcat on my hands. She could screw for England and had the most amazing pair of boobs. Marie said that Len had a massive dick and certainly knew how to use it. "Must be all the practice they get with each other," I said.

We laughed as we drove out of their ramshackle farmyard with its overgrown vegetation and bits of obsolete tractor parts strewn around. But we were both glad to be away from the dark and depressing atmosphere of the house. There was something not right about the place and we never went back or spoke to them again.

During our journeys we ran into a couple from Banbury who told us about a select group of couples who met regularly at a local, converted barn. It seems they only let new members into the circle if they could pass a test. This intrigued us and after a bit of detective work and half a dozen phone calls, we found ourselves talking on the telephone to members of the Sugar Candy club as they called it. We were told that very few new couples were allowed into the club but if we sent a photo of ourselves (undressed) to prove that we were attractive then we may be allowed to take the test to gain membership. The couple declined to tell us what the test entailed, only that it involved stamina and willpower.

We loved all the cloak and dagger stuff and duly sent two photos of ourselves (naked of course) to a P.0. Box in Banbury. We knew it could all be an elaborate plan to collect photos, but at that time we didn't worry about minor details. We were caught up in the game and just out to have fun.

Within a week our photos were returned, with a letter saying we had been granted permission to take the test. A week later we were met outside an old world pub in Banbury by a couple who ushered us into their car. They said they would take us to the converted barn where we would be put to the test. As we drove along the pleasant country lanes of middle England I began to have second thoughts. These people could be devil worshippers or axe murderers and we're sat in the back of their car, without a clue where we were going or what awaited us.

At that moment I realized that we had to slow our hectic lifestyle of the past year or we could eventually end up in a situation that we could not control and not escape from.

Until now, we had considered ourselves almost indestructible and had become immune to the strange and sometimes dangerous situations that we'd found ourselves in. It was now time to rein back and be more selective of the people we met. If not, we may not survive another year. If we make it through this, I told myself, we will reassess our lifestyle and get things into perspective.

We had been driving for about ten minutes when the car swung down a narrow lane, which led onto an open courtyard, at the end of which stood the much-heralded converted barn. It was smaller than I had expected, not much bigger than a normal semi but the renovations had maintained the original oak beams, which gave it, at first glance, a Tudor look.

We were met at the door by the couple we had spoken to on the phone who, it turned out, owned the barn and had founded the Sugar Candy Club for the more discerning swinger. I had to smile when I heard that because, if there was one thing we were not at that time it was discerning. We still did not know the names of our hosts but they were an attractive couple in their late forties and dressed casually but tastefully.

"Please come this way," said our host, as he led us over the cobbled courtyard towards the knarled oak door of the barn. Inside were ten other couples, all dressed in the same casual and conservative way. They greeted us in a friendly manner and offered us a drink. The conversation, though, was superficial and they were giving nothing away as we did our best to question them about the test. But at least I felt relieved that I couldn't see any pentangles drawn on the floor and no one was dressed in robes or carried flaming torches.

After about twenty minutes of polite conversation our hostess suddenly asked, "Are you ready to take the test?"

"What do we have to do?" I said.

"It's what you don't have to do that matters," she answered, with a smile. "Would you come with me?"

We left the other couples and followed the founders into an adjoining room. On the floor had been spread six double-size mattresses that almost covered the entire floor space.

"In five minutes all the couples you met outside will come into this room. They will all be naked," said our host.

"It's going to be an orgy?" Marie asked.

"No," said the man. Turning to me, "You, Barry, will be the test subject of the women, who will do their best to make you come. Your test is to stop yourself from ejaculating for half an hour."

"Ten, beautiful, naked women trying to make me come, and all I have to do is keep from shooting my load for half an hour," I exclaimed. "Couldn't you give me something a little easier, like emptying Loch Ness with a teaspoon?"

Our host smiled and turned to Marie, "Your task Marie, will be to make all ten men ejaculate in half an hour, but I warn you they will be doing their best to resist. If either one of you fail that will be the end of the test."

This was great, ten, beautiful, naked women all at once. Had I died and gone to heaven? Marie was smiling too, "Ten guys in half an hour," she said. "That's one every three minutes, no problem."

"Then let the test begin," said our host. Within seconds the couples were streaming into the room. Marie was undressing but I thought it better to keep my clothes on. It would help me stay in control and take up valuable time as the ladies tried to undress me. Two of them pushed me back onto the mattress and began pulling my trousers off. Another started to French kiss me, as more joined in, rubbing their hands over my body.

There was a clock on the wall that I kept an eagle eye on. It had been nine o'clock when we began but only a couple of minutes had passed before they had me naked. I did my best to talk to them but they would not be sidetracked and began fondling me. By five past, I had a raging hard on and was ready to come.

Marie, who had a dick in each hand, glanced over and, seeing me about to surrender, shouted out, "Barry, think of football." I came to my senses just in time and concentrated hard on my beloved Blades. Now I have to say, as much as I love football, there is nothing remotely sexy about twenty-two hairy, sweaty blokes running around kicking lumps out of each other. It did the trick. I began to lose my erection. It was ten past, I still had twenty minutes to survive without coming, surrounded by ten sex, mad women. I didn't think even Sheffield United could help me for that long, especially as one of the girls was now straddling my face and another was playing with her breasts. I strained to look sideways where I could see Marie had just successfully brought another guy off. I think it was her fourth. It was now quarter past and I was on the point of coming again, and, more to the point, not caring. I was being sucked by at least three women all taking turns, two more were kissing me and another three or four were doing the whole girly thing with each other, as a side show.

"I can't hold it, I can't hold it," I shouted. Marie

ceased sucking on a guy's cock just long enough to shout, "Remember Kenny and June." The sudden image of those horrible grins and the memory of that awful night was enough to knock the edge off my impending climax and pull me back from the brink of failure.

Marie was pulling out all the stops and had dispensed with another three guys by the time the clock read twenty past. Only ten minutes to go and I felt confident that between them Sheffield United and Kenny and June would see me through. I now had Kenny playing centre forward with June in goal and it was working a treat as we came up to injury time. But I still had a good hard on and if my concentration slipped for one second I would explode like a firecracker. It was twenty-five minutes past nine when the blonde with the big boobs impaled herself on me. I was on my back and she sat astride me with two other women, either side of her, gripping her arms and lifting her up and down. I knew I was doomed when I heard her scream, "I'm coming, I'm coming." As she writhed around, I couldn't hold out any longer as I exploded inside her.

As soon as I had stopped jerking, I screamed out, "Oh no, just three minutes to go. I can't believe it."

Marie was down to her last man, but he was having none of it. I could see she was tiring as she had to change hands every so often, which broke the rhythm, and the guy had an iron will because he never lost his concentration. He must have been an Oxford supporter as they are the only team who are even less sexy than the Blades. Half past came. We had both failed. It had been fun but Marie had only made nine out of ten ejaculate and I had come with just three minutes left on the clock.

We were apologizing to everyone but they just laughed and kept patting us on the back and congratulating us. When our host couple entered the room, they seemed happy. "You have passed the test," said the man.

"But we didn't make the time limit," I answered.

"Yes you did," said his wife. "If you had held out, it would have told us you were not horny enough for our club. You see, we like our members to surrender to their feelings, not keep them in check."

"But what about me?" asked Marie. "I couldn't get the man to come in the time allowed."

"You were fantastic," said the women. "All the guys had masturbated already, half an hour before you got here, so the fact you made nine of them come again proves you are an extremely horny woman. You can consider yourself members of the Sugar Candy Club."

The club had about forty couples, but whenever a new couple wanted to join, they would dream up an initiation ceremony. They had decided on ours a week before we travelled down to Banbury. It all added to the fun and none of it was taken seriously. We were involved in the initiation of a couple from London who, it was decided, would have to meet and screw five different couples in five different secluded parts of Banbury in under ninety minutes. We were to be the fifth couple and we waited in our car in a quiet lay-by for eighty minutes before they arrived, looking totally dishevelled, but they still managed to perform reasonably well for the last ten minutes and passed the test.

The Sugar Candy Club was all about the feeling of belonging to a select group of people, and it felt good to be part of something which had rules and etiquette, and high standards of behaviour. It helped steady us down and taught us restraint. It did not last though, as within a year of us becoming members, the Sugar Candy Club had grown to more than one hundred and fifty couples and the inevitable squabbles and in-fighting began to erode the high standards the club had started out with and it broke up. But it was fun while it lasted and it gave us a sense of belonging and status that we put to good use many years later when we opened our own up-market venue for swingers.

With the demise of Sugar Candy we were able to take stock of our lives and look for new directions. We stringently vetted the new couples we came in contact with and, if there was the slightest doubt in either of us, then we would not take it further.

We were no longer screwing people just for the hell of it, we were moving into a new stage of our development. Our wild days were over and now we would seek and value friendship and compatibility, as much as we had once sought lustful gratification.

CHAPTER 8

The Hound of St Albans

The old house was undeniably impressive; it was Victorian, three stories high and built from granite stone. Streams of ivy interlaced the panelled sash windows, and above the colossal front door, elaborately carved into the stone lintel, was a coat of arms. Inscribed underneath was the motto, 'For Perfection We Strive'. This brought a wry smile to my face, considering why we were here. The house stood on a tree-lined avenue on the outskirts of St. Albans. We had parked across the road, the four of us, Marie, myself, and Danny and Sue, a couple we had got to know very well over the last few months. They were about the same age as us and, with a young family similar to our own, we had much in common. We had swung together on half a dozen occasions and enjoyed each other's company.

Danny was a ruggedly handsome, Irishman with a shock of unruly, black, curly hair and a perpetual smile on his face. He was a soundproofer by trade, which was ironic because he had the loudest voice I had ever heard. Even one of Danny's whispers could be heard on the other side of a noisy bar. On more than one occasion,

Danny's vocal observations on the size of some woman's breasts in a pub had led to us beating a hasty retreat. It had got to a point where, to save ourselves embarrassment, not to mention the growing likelihood of being beaten up, we would arrange to meet them in non-public places.

But Danny was tremendous fun, and the fact that Marie rated him as a good screw more than made up for his occasional vocal indiscretions. Also in the good screw category was Sue, Danny's wife. With her dark shoulder-length hair and love of leather, she was a Suzi Quatro look-alike, the female rock singer who was all the rage at that time. So it was inevitable that we would nickname her Suzi Q. Sue's only downfall was her reaction to red wine. She loved the stuff, but unfortunately it did not love her, and one glass full was enough to make her violently ill. So it was in the back of my mind that we would have to keep a close watch on Suzi Q once inside the house.

Now, house parties can be tremendous fun or complete disasters, because you never really know what you're letting yourself in for until it's too late. But that unpredictability is part of the attraction and, when Danny had heard, via the grapevine, that there was to be a big bash at a posh drum in St. Albans, we had all jumped at the chance. Marie and I had been swinging for over three years by this time and were well passed the stomach, churning nervousness we used to feel when meeting a new couple or going to a house party. Of course the old buzz of excitement was still there, that never leaves you. But now we had the added problem of Danny's voice and public places, always a volatile mix, and Sue's addiction to red wine, and so it was with a mixture of excitement and some trepidation that we crossed the leaf-strewn road and knocked on the majestic-looking front door.

The door opened to reveal a tall, thin, aristocratic-looking man in his early fifties. Beside him stood a huge Afghan hound. Just for a moment as they stood together framed in the hallway light man and dog looked identical, both aloof, both superior, both hawk-like in appearance.

"Hello, this is the right place for the house party?" I asked. I had to resist the urge to tug my forelock as I spoke. A smile bisected his long bony features.

"It is indeed!" he exclaimed. "Do come in. My name is Julian and I'm your host. Please come through to the lounge and meet the others."

His accent was pure BBC-newsreader English. We followed him, and the Afghan, into a large lounge where at least ten other couples were already chatting amicably. The room itself had the air of a Victorian sifting room, full of period furniture and tastefully decorated.

There were three, full-size, green leather Chesterfield settees in a semi-circle around a splendid, ornate fireplace in which crackled a real log fire. A luxurious sheepskin rug was spread seductively between the Chesterfields. Soft music and subdued lighting completed the scene.

Apart from the people in the lounge, I could see another two or three couples in the kitchen that ran off next to the lounge. It was all very civilized and refined. At that moment, Julian announced that two of the couples present were incredibly nervous because they were first timers and could everyone go easy on them.

Danny's response was frighteningly predictable. He leaned next to my ear and in a loud whisper said, "Did you hear that, Baz, fresh meat."

A stunned silence descended on the room. Marie squeezed my hand so hard I thought she would break my fingers. I felt a sickly smile spread across my face. One of the first-time couples laughed nervously, and Julian saved the day by turning up the volume on the stereo, and feverishly freshening everyone's drink. As nonchalantly as I could I sat on the arm of one of the Chesterfields, next to a pretentious-looking woman in a red lace top. As I sat down she moved away markedly, a curl of her lip making it obvious that she considered our presence to have lowered the tone of the gathering. Marie and Suzi Q had wandered off to get a drink but out of the corner of my eye I could see Danny moving towards me. I knew instinctively he was going to say something insulting about the snotty woman, and I also knew that, even though he thought he was whispering, everyone in the room would hear.

I gritted my teeth and prayed for death. Mercifully a loud peal of laughter emerged from the kitchen as Danny's words echoed in my ear. "Who does she think she is, the fucking Queen of Sheba?" A quick glance around the room told me that miraculously no-one seemed to have heard Danny this time; except, that is for the Queen of Sheba herself.

She looked up sharply, her steely blue eyes narrowing to mere slits and her thin lips pursed into a vicious ball of wrinkles. I thought it prudent at this stage to retreat swiftly. I could feel her glare burning into my back as I bustled Danny into the kitchen, where we found a couple of cool lagers and I pondered the wisdom of accompanying Danny and Sue to a big house party. But at least for the moment we were out of harm's way.

Over the next twenty minutes another dozen or so couples arrived. Marie and Suzi Q were now smooching with the two new guys, while their wives sat huddled together looking terrified. The Queen of Sheba had been knocking back huge quantities of vodka and orange, and was now dancing topless to Hot Chocolate's 'You Sexy Thing'. Couples were beginning to pair off and disappear upstairs.

At that moment, the Afghan hound burst though the lounge slammed into one of the Chesterfields and galloped into the kitchen. Where it proceeded to bound crazily from one end of the room to the other, it's great pink tongue slapping from side to side, sending long tendrils of saliva arcing through the air. Danny and I watched in amazement as the huge, hairy canine seized a pair of lace panties, that had been hanging on the back of a chair by the gusset. It shook them from side to side so violently that its rear end seemed to be becoming detached from the rest of its body.

Suddenly it froze and fixed us with a vacant stare, the panties still hanging from its quivering jaw. Then, just as suddenly, it galloped off again through the lounge and up the stairs. "Now there goes a dog on the edge," said Danny, wiping a strand of saliva from his lower leg. -

"I think he may have gone over the edge," I answered, feeling relieved that I seemed to have escaped the saliva shower unscathed.

"Right I'm off upstairs to see what the girls are up to. Coming, Baz?"

"I'll follow you up soon, mate," I said, running my fingers through my hair and finding I hadn't escaped the shower of saliva after all.

I had hesitated because I had noticed a buxom blonde sitting alone and semi-naked on the rug by the fire. So, leaving Danny to wander upstairs, I sauntered over and stood next to her. "Hi, my name is Barry. What's yours?" I asked.

She looked up slowly, and with eyes that seemed to be swimming in alcohol, desperately tried to focus on me. After a few seconds she gave up and, with as much dignity as she could muster, said, "scuse me but would you like to fuck?"

"Why how kind of you to ask, I believe I would," I replied and sat down beside her on the sheepskin rug. Within seconds she had inserted her hand between my legs and thrust her tongue down my throat. Now call it instinct, intuition, or just a gut feeling, but something told me I could definitely skip the foreplay with blondie.

By now the party was in full flow and moans and groans interlaced with shrieks of laughter were emanating from all corners of the house. Every now and then I would hear a crash as a glass or bottle was knocked over, followed by a loud whoopee or whatever noise drunken people make when something is broken.

I was really getting into it with blondie on the sheepskin rug when I heard Danny's distinctive, booming voice echoing from upstairs. "Baz, Baz, come and look at this quick." It sounded urgent and, fearing some kind of trouble, I hastily extracted myself from Blondie's clutches and ran into the hallway. Danny was standing at the top of the stairs, naked and bouncing around with excitement. "Baz, you've got to see this. the Afghan is shagging the Queen of Sheba."

I bounded up the stairs two at a time. Danny hustled me into a bedroom to the left of the landing and there, on the bed, on all fours giving a guy oral was the Queen of Sheba, with the Afghan hound clamped to her back, its rear end going like the clappers.

"She's pissed as a fart," howled Danny. "She thinks its some guy." He was laughing so much I thought he would have a heart attack. There were about five or six other people in the room, all drunk to varying degrees.

A couple of them began to chant, "Go Rover, Go Rover," another put a pillow behind the back legs of the Afghan as he seemed to be loosing his grip on the cotton bed sheets.

In between shrieks of laughter, Danny was shouting out scores, "Nine out of ten for technique, ha ha. Seven out of ten for artistic merit, ha ha ha. Oh he slipped a bit there, but I don't think the judges will hold it against him, ha ha, ha ha." Danny was now laughing so much he had turned bright red and was pounding the floor to get his breath.

I really had to admire the big dog's style, and his stamina was formidable. His head lay flat on the Queen's back, and if I hadn't known better I could have sworn he had a smile on his big, hairy face. He kept trying to nip the back of the Queen's neck but because she had her head forward, giving the guy a blow job, he couldn't get a hold and kept slipping back. The whole scene had a surreal quality about it.

Suddenly from behind us came an anguished yell. It was Mr. Sheba. A look of horror engulfed his face, and he promptly turned on his heels and ran down the stairs. Now that's strange I thought. His wife is up here being back scuttled by an Afghan hound, so why is he running down stairs? I had my answer moments later, when he came bounding back up the stairs with a carving knife in his hand, screaming that he was going to kill the dog.

It was at that point that our host, Julian, appeared at the top of the landing, wearing just his socks and a bow tie. "What's going on?" he demanded.

"I'm going to stab your fucking dog," growled Mr. Sheba.

"Marmaduke, you're trying to stab Marmaduke. You're a madman," Julian screamed.

Within seconds Julian and Mr. Sheba began wrestling at the top of the stairs. Now Danny, who had only just managed to get his breath back after his laughing fit, immediately dissolved into hysterical laughter once again.

"Fuck me, Marmaduke. Did you hear that, Baz? They call the fucking dog Marmaduke, ha ha ha ha." He fell into a crumpled heap, laughing uncontrollably.

By this time my mind was reeling. I had Danny to one side of me totally out of control and helpless; to the other side two naked men were having a knife fight, and to top it all, I had no idea where the girls were. What else could possible go wrong? That was when I heard Marie calling to me from downstairs. "Barry, come quickly. Sue's been on the red wine."

Now there are very rare occasions, perhaps only once or twice in a lifetime, when even though chaos reigns all around you, your mind becomes infinitely focused. Everything is crystal clear and you know exactly what to do. Unfortunately for me, this was not one of them. I didn't have a clue, in fact the proverbial rock and the hard place looked positively inviting compared to this situation.

My first problem was to get myself and Danny past the two naked gladiators at the top of the stairs, without losing any bodily parts, a task made doubly difficult as Danny had now drifted into a drunken stupor after exhausting himself laughing. But for the first time that night, luck was with me as the two warriors lurched to one side of the landing.

I grabbed Danny and half staggered, half fell down the stairs. As we entered the kitchen, I was met with the sight of Suzi Q projectile-vomiting across the kitchen floor. Marie was soaked in second-hand red wine and feebly holding what looked like a soggy towel up to Suzie's face, in a vain attempt to quell the next expulsion.

"We have got to get out of here," she hissed. This was a sentiment I shared whole-heartedly, but there was another problem. We were all naked and had no idea where our clothes were. So for the next few minutes Marie and I scoured the kitchen and lounge for items of clothing, not necessarily our own, anything so we would not have to drive home naked. Danny actually wore a cute little sequined tank-top all the way back up the Ml. Miraculously, I managed to find my trousers containing the car keys. They were next to the sheepskin rug where blondie had unceremoniously dragged them off me earlier. I ran into the kitchen and held them up triumphantly. Just in time for a plume of vomit to engulf my right hand and trousers in the process. "There can't be much left in her," said Marie.

"No, it's all in my trouser pockets," I said, as I gingerly extracted the soggy keys with my dry hand.

Eventually the four of us staggered into the hallway. The battle between Julian and Mr. Sheba had grown in intensity and now involved at least a dozen combatants, who were beginning to spill down the stairs.

We swung open the front door and somehow crossed the tree-lined avenue and dumped Sue and Danny into the back seat of the car. Before clambering in ourselves, we took one last look at the house. The lights on the first floor were flickering on and off. We heard a loud crash, a dog bark, and a woman scream. We dived in the car, I wheel spun along the avenue and headed for home. Mercifully Sue had stopped vomiting and was snoring loudly on the back seat. Danny was semi-conscious and muttering something about Marmaduke being his hero. We drove in stunned silence for a while until Marie spoke,

"If ever there was a night to forget this is it." I agreed, but suspected it would be a night we would remember for a very long time indeed.

CHAPTER 9

The Doggers

In the hills above the picturesque North Derbyshire town of Mattock is a car park. In summer by day it is packed with picnicking families and tourists who flock to the area for the magnificent scenery. By night it becomes a hive of sexual activity, populated by exhibitionist swingers and doggers.

'Dogging' is a term that originated in the early seventies to describe men who spied on couples having nookie outdoors. These men would dog the couple's every move in an effort to watch them screw, and when the swinging scene discovered that open air sex has its own special thrill and began to meet in car parks, the doggers found a new and rich supply of voyeuristic fun. Better still, they soon realised that these couples actively encouraged their voyeurism, even performing for them. Within a few short years a whole new culture had grown around car park fun. Dozens of secluded car parks, all over the country, had become regular meeting places for swingers and their dogger entourage. The one on the hills over Mattock was well suited to this new and exciting pastime, being surrounded by thick undergrowth and the only entrance and exit being a narrow lane from the main road about two hundred yards long.

The downside to car park fun is that it's illegal, the charge being one of 'lewd behaviour in a public place', but of course you have to be actually caught having sex or indulging in sexual activities to be charged. So the long lane leading to the hilltop car park served a dual purpose. Not only was it the only way in and out, but you could see any headlights turning off the main road a good minute or so before they entered the car park. The only problem being that it was impossible to tell if it was a police car or not until it reached the entrance.

I have to say, in all the years we have engaged in car park fun I have never yet seen a police car enter one, or heard of anyone who has been arrested. I am sure the police know of them but take the view that they present no threat to the public. After all, the people who frequent them are not there to steal or hurt anyone, and by the nature of what it entails the car parks are chosen for their remoteness. I would think also that the police would welcome anything that draws the peeping toms away from the public at large. The exhibitionist couples are not going to complain about being watched, that's the reason they are there and the doggers are hardly likely to cause trouble for fear of ruining their voyeuristic fun. So the symbiotic relationship between swingers and doggers works because each supplies something the other needs.

We had indulged in car park fun periodically for a few years, the scenario being we would turn up, usually with another couple, park up and switch on the interior light. We would then start to undress in the car. As soon as the girls got down to their bras and panties you could guarantee there would be ten to fifteen doggers, creeping out from the bushes to watch. Mostly we would go with Danny and Sue, who were always up for a laugh. Danny and I loved to let Sue and Marie put on a two-girl show in the back seat. That really used to drive the Doggers crazy. They would come up to the window and ask if they could stick their dicks in so the girls could masturbate them, but we always said no, that would be far too messy inside the car.

On average, there would be eight or nine couples performing at any one time and perhaps twenty or thirty doggers. Some couples would screw on the bonnet of their car and the doggers would illuminate the scene by shining their headlights at them. A few couples would let selected doggers join in, with the lucky ones managing to get a screw. Mostly though they were there as voyeurs, and got their kicks by watching.

We would see many of the same faces whenever we went and the regular doggers began to acquire nicknames. All the couples knew them by these names. You would here a couple saying something like where's Black beard tonight? Or we haven't seen Bent dick for the last couple of months. Another dogger who earned his name the hard way was Tarzan. He could always be found up a tree and would spend the whole night up there, scanning the car park from his lofty vantage point with binoculars, only coming down when the last couple had left. The Screamer was one of the best-known doggers at that time. He was in his late twenties and exceptionally tall and thin with a bent back. He would creep up to a car to watch the activities and begin to masturbate. Faster and faster he would wank until he climaxed, at which time he would let out the most incredible, high- pitched scream. This was sure to kill all sexual activity for the next twenty minutes or so, as everyone would be in fits of laughter. Once his screaming had ceased and he had come to his senses, he would skulk away, climb in his V. W. Beetle and drive off. We did hear that he used to frequent another car park down Birmingham way, where he was known as The Banshee.

Probably the best known of all the doggers at the Matlock car park was Curly, so called because he was completely bald. Curly must have been going on for eighty and he always wore an old, grey overcoat that looked at best two sizes too big for him. He was always there, trying to get in on some action, but of course none of the women would let him get anywhere near them, so he had to be content with being on the edge of things. One particular night turned out to be very traumatic for Curly and almost cost him his life.

It was a warm night, with a full moon and a few of the doggers were jittery because someone had supposedly seen a police car cruising the main road. So no sooner had the action started than a set of headlights would be seen coming down the lane, and one of the doggers would shout "police car" and the whole lot of them would disappear into the undergrowth. Leaving the couples to quickly re arrange their clothing and pick up a map book or break out the sandwiches. Heaven knows what the police would have made of a dozen or so couples sat reading road maps or eating sandwiches in a remote hilltop car park at 1 o'clock in the morning, to say nothing of the twenty odd empty cars parked up around the edges.

Thankfully it never happened, but as I say, this night the doggers were on edge and poor old Curly was slower than the rest, so by the time the all-clear was given, he was still trying to get his breath back from the dash for cover. Danny would call out to him, as the doggers returned after a dash, "Come in, Curly, your time is up." This was always followed by a loud cheer, as he tentatively peeped from the undergrowth, always a good few minutes after everyone else had crept back.

That night, at least four couples had grown tired of the continued interruptions and left, but we decided to give it one more try. So Marie and Sue got out of the car and started to kiss and fondle each other whilst sat on the bonnet. This had the desired effect as they were soon surrounded by a posse of doggers.

As usual, Danny was having a great time, "Line up there, gents, no need to push. There's room for everyone. Please don't wank on the paintwork." Danny loved the idea of winding the guys up and then sending them on their way. Of course you may think that this is a dangerous thing to do seeing as there were about twenty of them and only two of us. They could easily overpower us and do what they wanted to the girls, but it does not work that way. The doggers are highly organised, and know that any such action would result in all the swinging couples deserting the car park scene, and that would be the end of the fun for everyone. Indeed the odd times that anyone got out of line, they were usually dealt with by the doggers themselves. It has been known for a dogger to be beaten up as punishment for upsetting a couple. It is by no means common, but it does happen and the couples feel safer for it. So neither Danny nor I were in any danger and, for the most part, the doggers took Danny's ribbing in good heart.

"Roll up, roll up chaps. See the two naked ladies finger-fuck each other. Masturbate yourselves if you must. The first one to come gets an orange."

At that Sue and Marie burst out laughing and almost fell off the bonnet. The big Irishman had turned the little show into a comedy; even some of the doggers were chuckling to themselves.

Danny continued, "Hey, Tarzan, are you up there? If you are, throw us a coconut down. I'm thirsty."

To Danny's surprise a little voice came back at him from somewhere high up in the trees, "Fuck off."

"Well, I'm shocked and appalled," shouted Danny. "Is that the kind of language the apes are teaching now days?"

The whole car park seemed to erupt with laughter. Danny stood, shaking his head in mock indignation.

"Come on, Tarzan. Fart and give us a clue where you are."

Many of the doggers were doubled up with laughter and seemed to be enjoying the show so much they had forgotten why they were there.

"Bollocks," replied the little voice from the trees.

"Ah, such a wide and varied vocabulary," Danny replied. "Have you ever considered lecturing on grammar at university?"

Everyone was now enthralled by this bizarre conversation between the loud and jovial Irishman and the disembodied voice, emanating down from the treetops. An expectant hush fell upon the gathering, as they waited for Tarzan's response to Danny's taunt. Seconds passed. All was quiet; it could only mean Tarzan was composing a witty put-down for Danny. More seconds, then it came, carried down from the lofty heights on the hint of a summer breeze. "Get fucked."

A howl of laughter engulfed the car park. It was so loud a flock of birds suddenly rose from one of the trees, screeching their disapproval at being woken from their sleep.

Just as I was wondering what Danny would say next, headlights could be seen turning off the main road and on to the narrow lane. Panic swept through the ranks of the doggers again, as the shout went up, "It's a raid, go, go, go." Within seconds the whole group had gone crashing into the undergrowth. As usual Curly was last to disappear, but I could see he was gathering speed as he vanished into the tree line,

his long grey overcoat ballooning behind him like a half-open parachute, his shrunken, naked body glowing white, like a living skeleton in the moonlight." I've never seen Curly run so fast," I said.

"Yeah, those little legs of his were just a blur," answered Danny. The girls had already thrown on their coats and were studying a road map when the headlights flashed into the car park. It was another dogger, arriving late.

A collective groan went up from the remaining couples and slowly the doggers began to re-emerge from the foliage. They would creep out looking furtive and then remonstrate with the late arrival for disturbing the action. Although on this night it wasn't so much sexual action that had been interrupted as a comedy show, but for now at least Tarzan was keeping quiet. He had been verbally thrashed by Danny and was laying low, or at least as low as you can lay in the top of a tree.

Eventually the doggers had all reassembled and pockets of conversation began to develop.

Then someone asked, "Where's Curly?"

Everyone looked around. He was nowhere to be seen. It had been over fifteen minutes since the last panic and Curly had not reappeared. His tatty, old Morris Minor was still parked up near the entrance so he had not left. He must still be in the undergrowth somewhere.

It was decided we would all spread out to look for him. Danny and I made for the place where we had seen him hurtling into the trees when the last dash occurred. It was thick undergrowth, full of bracken and hawthorns. We could just make out a trail of broken twigs and stems, where Curly had rampaged through in his panic.

"Jesus, he must have been going like a train, to leave a trail like this," said Danny. On we went into the dense tangle of branches. It was almost pitch black in there, even with the moonlight. It was difficult to make out shapes in the thick shrubbery.

Then we heard it, a tiny plaintive voice, "Help, help." It was Curly.

"Where are you?" I shouted.

"Over here. Help me please I'm stuck." We followed the sound of his feeble voice.

"Where are you stuck?" I asked.

"In a bush. I'm stuck in a bush," Curly answered.

I turned to Danny. "Did he say in a bush?"

"He did that," Danny answered.

"Keep talking," I said. "We'll find you."

"I'm over here, in the middle of this bush. Please help me." We made our way over to a large hawthorn bush and there, in the middle hung Curly, grotesquely caught up in its thorny branches.

By now, we had been joined by two or three of the doggers. One of them had a torch and, as he shone it at Curly, we could see what had happened. In his panic-stricken dash for safety, he had slammed into the bush at a rate of knots so great he had become embedded in its centre. He was frozen in a sort of running position, entangled so tight it was impossible for him to go forward or back. His overcoat was snagged behind him, looking like a cape caught in the wind.

Another dogger joined us. "He's in the bush!" he said incredulously.

"That's right," I answered. "He's in the bush."

"I've never seen anybody stuck in a bush before," he said, peering at the forlorn figure of Curly.

"I must admit it's a first for me too," I said. "But the question is how do we get him out? Has anybody got any garden shears?" said the dogger.

"Oh yes," said Danny. "It just so happens that in my pocket."

"I know," said another dogger, interrupting Danny's sarcasm. "We'll drag him out by pulling on his coat."

"I don't think that's such a good idea," I said. "The thorns are already sticking in him. If we try to pull him out he'll be shredded."

"You're right there Baz, so you are," said Danny. "He'll be shredded for sure." This brought a fresh groan of despair from Curly.

"Please help me I can't feel my feet, and I think I'm bleeding." We shone the torch over Curly's naked body, and sure enough he had several deep lacerations, a couple of which would obviously need stitches.

"Right, there's only one thing for it," I said. "If we all take our shirts or jumpers off and wrap them around our arms, we can force the branches back andease him out."

"Right you lot, you heard the man. Off with your shirts," shouted Danny sergeant-major fashion. The doggers must have all been ex-squaddies because they obeyed Danny's orders without question.

Within a couple of minutes we had fought our way to the centre of the bush and had begun to extract Curly. Inch by inch, we pulled and twisted him from the spiky grip of the hawthorn bush. His shrieks of pain split the air, as thorns were plucked from his skin before the next movement could commence.

Eventually he was out, "Oh God bless you. God bless you boys," he repeated over and over as we carried him out of the undergrowth and into the car park. We lifted him over to his car and laid him on the bonnet.

"Let's have a look at him," I said. "Where's the torch?"

In the beam we could see the extent of Curly's injuries. Scratches, grazes and cuts littered his skinny little body. Poor old Curly was groaning pathetically as a posse of would-be doctors and nurses gave their diagnosis and instigated a compilation of impromptu treatments.

Suddenly Danny, who had been inspecting Curly's body with a look of disgust on his face, let out a yell. "Aargh look at his dick."

"What's up with it?" I said.

"It's all wrinkly," Danny blurted. "It's all skin. I don't think there's really a dick in there, its all just wrinkly skin."

"It's because he's old," I said. "Anyway, I don't think his wrinkly dick is his main problem just now." But Danny would not be sidetracked.

"I just hope my dick doesn't look like that when I get old. It's horrible, no wonder he keeps that long coat on all the time. It's to hide his dick."

Many of the couples and doggers were now keenly inspecting Curly's wrinkled dick, after which a discussion ensued, where it was universally agreed that Curly's dick was indeed horrible.

Curly was still spread-eagled on the bonnet of his old Morris Minor, with his head propped up on the windscreen and his spindly, little legs dangling over the radiator grill. Smears of blood covered his pale skin and he hardly had the strength to lift one arm.

Just then another set of headlights turned into the top of the lane.

"It's the coppers," somebody screamed and everyone scattered, leaving Curly lying there on the bonnet of his car. The young couple in the car didn't have a clue what was going on, as their headlights lit up the prone and bloodied body of Curly on his bonnet. It must have looked like some hideous vigilante justice, as they screeched to a halt and then sped back up the lane, sending showers of dirt and gravel everywhere in their desperation to escape.

Curly was eventually taken to hospital and left in casualty by one of the doggers and within a month was back at the car park, none the worse for his adventure. Never was a man more dedicated to his hobby.

The car park scene is today more widespread than ever and far more organised. Some groups of doggers even use walkie-talkies and two-way radios to communicate and tell each other where the best action is happening. And coded newspaper ads and internet websites keep the modern doggers up to date with the latest news on where to find the best car park fun. It's all a far cry from the days of Black beard, Bent dick, Tarzan and Screamer. Perhaps they have their present-day counterparts but surely there can only be one Curly? And if he is now in that big car park in the sky, I wish him good viewing, and may all the bushes have soft thorns.

The photograph of Marie which we sent out and received an enormous response.

Barry in the gym in the early eighties.

Marie pre-eighties before we started swinging.

Marie posing for the camera 1985

Barry and Marie relaxing at home in 1985.

CHAPTER 10

How It Works

There is a great mystery concerning the swinging scene. As in most things, ignorance is the real problem and as swinging is seen as taboo by the majority of the population (at least in public) ignorance rules supreme, and where ignorance rules, fear is never far away. That is why the vast majority of the non-swinging population will vehemently attack and vilify anyone who admits to being a swinger. Perverts, weirdos, depraved, these are all common words that are used to describe swingers. The abuse sometimes borders on the fanatical in its intensity. In fact it seems that child molesters and rapists do not attract as much scathing abuse as swingers. Why should this be, when basically swinging is all about consenting adults having fun with the knowledge and blessing of their partner?

The answer, of course, is fear. Swinging is honest, there is no subterfuge involved, no lying or clandestine meetings, no cheating on your partner. This is the paradox for most non-swingers. We are taught that sex with anyone who is not your partner is wrong and so must be kept a secret. The secrecy somehow cleanses the act of adultery for the non-swinger; so, rather than not commit adultery at all, they will seek to hide the act, and in doing so, appease their guilt. They fear the honesty of the swinger.

It flies in the face of tradition and breaks all the rules. It undermines the tried and tested method of cheating on your partner. It's just not British. Of course, there are many people who have never cheated on their partners and some of these are the worst of all in their intense hatred of swingers. Because they feel pure at heart they seek to command the moral high ground and deem themselves ultimately qualified to condemn anyone who does not fall into their tunnel view of the world. They would happily have all swingers burned at the stake as spawn of the Devil for daring to question the outdated, moralistic rules by which they live. These couples have placed the act of sex on a pedestal so high that very often they themselves cannot reach it.

The ability to enjoy sex, as more than a means to maintain the species, is one of the elements that differentiates us from animals, but then we hinder that element by placing moralistic rules on our enjoyment, which destroys the whole damn thing. So we either, break the rules, like the vast majority of the adult population and suffer the guilt and pain of deception, or we do not agree with the rules, thus freeing ourselves from all the emotive baggage connected with rule-breaking and become a swinger.

Ninety-nine percent of men and eighty percent of all women would admit to wanting sex with people other than their partner if they were totally honest, but honesty is the first casualty when the chance for casual sex comes along. and that is sad, not just because society forces us to decide whether we cheat on our partner or live a frustrating monogamous life, but because it does not have to be that way.

Sex should be taken from its altar and cease to be revered as the ultimate expression of love. You do not have to love someone to have sex with them. Love transcends the physical act of sex. It is too easy to mix them up and believe that they are one and the same. They are not. You can love someone with all your heart and still want sex with others. It's natural, it's human, in many cultures of the world it's expected.

The conflict lies between genetics and indoctrination. What we feel in the core of our DNA, and what we have been taught to believe by a society that takes its doctrine from long-dead religious zealots, who sought to control the masses by imposing moralistic rules that if broken, carried the death penalty. If those penalties were still in force today the vast majority of the population would have been stoned to death long ago. Of course the rules are still in place but now our punishment is shame and guilt.

But more and more people are questioning those rules and are struggling to tell fact from fiction. For them swinging offers a way out, but it can seem like a minefield to the uninitiated.

Many myths and untruths flourish because of rumors, but like most things, it's easy once you know how.

In the early eighties, contact with another couple was made in one of two ways. The first and by far the biggest were contact magazines. These were usually C5-size booklets packed with ads, some with pictures from couples and singles who wanted to meet with others of a like mind. A typical ad would read: Couple mid-thirties would like to meet other couples for ultimate fun. He straight, with dark hair and brown eyes, well hung. Her curvy, blonde hair, blue eyes and bi. ALA, photo appreciated, returned with ours.

This is the kind of ad we placed in the early days. It's pretty much run of the mill and would usually attract about a dozen return letters. As time went on, we would try to spice our ads up by putting something like:

If you want it come and get it. Good looking
couple, she bi, would like to meet same for adult fun
and erotic adventure. No timewasters please ALA.
Photo please.

This usually brought a response from the more serious players. We always used a photo of Marie in undies or even naked, photos always increase the response. Some letters that came back to us were short and to the point. One that we always remember was from an army sergeant and his wife based in Aldershot. It read:

We have seen your ad and would like to fuck you. If
you would like to fuck us please ring this number.

We gave that one a miss. Many of the couples who answer ads are time wasters or photo collectors. The time wasters will swap half a dozen sexy letters, maybe a few dirty phone calls and even make meeting arrangements but of course they will never turn up. They always have a good excuse though and will then attempt to go through the whole charade again. They get their kicks from the letters and phone calls and don't have the guts to actually meet people. These kind of couples can drive you insane. The photo collectors are simply that. They ask you to send undraped photos of yourselves with a promise that they will send them back with a photo of themselves by return. Of course, you never see theirs or yours again. We have lost hundreds of photos in this way. Many couples would resort to sending Photostat copies because they had lost so many photos. but the quality was often poor and it smacked of multiple submissions. We were always wary when we received Photostats. It told us the couple were scatter-gunning letters all over the place and were probably screwing anything that moved.

Then there are the single men, who pretend they are married in order to get into a couple. We drove up to Scotch Corner on the Great North road to meet a couple we had written to and seen photos of, only to find a single guy waiting. He said that his wife had been taken ill that evening and would it be ok if he performed with Marie while I watched. It took all of my self-control not to give him a whack, and after remonstrating with him in the car park he confessed that the photo he had sent us of his wife was actually a photo of a woman he had collected through the post from another couple.

So the percentage of genuine couples out of a bundle of say twelve letters could be as low as one or two, and even then, you both have to fancy them to arrange to meet up.

Marie has driven me crazy over the years because I will see a photo of a couple and think yes I could make it with her, only for Marie to announce that she does not fancy him. Women are far choosier than men, but then they can afford to be. They have all the power and they know it. They hold the veto over most meetings. They know that most men will want to screw almost any woman because men are driven by the insatiable desire that cruel Mother Nature has bestowed on them. Whereas most women only need to click their fingers and they will have a long line of willing men ready to service them. Consequently they can afford to be choosy or as Marie would say, more discerning.

So we have picked out a genuine couple and we both fancy them. The next step is to set up a meeting. It's always better to meet in a neutral place, a pub or club. It doesn't really matter, so long as no one has home advantage first time.

If you go to some-one's house, the pressure is on you to perform if they come onto you. Of course you can always tell them to back off, but it's an embarrassing situation and best avoided if you can. If you have people come to your house first time, you may not be able to get rid of them if they turn out to be morons.

Right, you have met a couple in a mutual place, now comes the crunch. How do we all get on? Remember our first experience with farmer Giles and Ginger. Are they what you expected? We met a couple we had spoken to on the telephone and exchanged a couple of letters with, and had formed the opinion that they were really friendly and something could come of it. In reality, within ten minutes of meeting them, we had decided that he was an arrogant, egotistical pig, and she was a stuck-up prima-donna. We have lost count of the number of couples who looked great in their photos and wrote lovely letters but were incapable of stringing two sentences together when we finally met them. It is far more difficult than you would imagine putting four people together and expecting them all to get on. There are four different personalities at work. It only takes one person to rock the boat and the whole group will fail to gel.

But let's say everyone gets on really well and fancy each other. There is one last step to overcome before they can get it together. What are their sexual preferences? Now you may think this is a strange question to ask, seeing as everyone is there for sex, but it's not always the case. Some couples only do same-room sex, some will only do separate room, others may just want a particular sexual act and nothing else.

Here is a prime example of being so near and yet so far. On meeting a great-looking couple from Oxford, I was chomping at the bit to get at this fantastic-looking redhead, even though she had stressed that she did not have intercourse with anyone but her partner, but she absolutely loved receiving and giving oral. I would happily forego intercourse just to experience the chance to taste her exquisite juices. But just as I was imagining my head between this beauty's curvy legs, she proceeded to tell us of the terrible bouts of thrush she regularly suffers and the awful discharge it gives her when it is really bad. That was one of the few times I have actually vetoed a possible meeting. Marie was really pissed off by that, as he was a real hunk. So you see nothing is as easy as it seems, but if you can get it together, boy is it worth the effort.

Word of mouth was the other way to meet couples back in the early eighties. If you knew a decent, genuine couple you would tell other genuine couples. In this way it kept all the timewasters out. Of course, today the Internet has revolutionized the swinging scene. There are literally hundreds of sites for swingers, with descriptions and photos readily available. Well-run adult clubs are now common place in Britain, many approaching continental standards where, like-minded adults can meet and have fun.

There are still contact magazines, although they are nowhere near as popular as they were, and some are nothing more than rip-offs, filled with false ads and asking for large payments for passing letters on, when in fact most letters end up in the bin.

As in most expanding activities, business has to a large degree taken over and money is the motivation behind most sex-related businesses. This is not always a bad thing, as standards have been raised considerably over the years in services and venues for liberated adults. Today's swingers will not stand for seedy clubs or poor service just because they enjoy sex. There is a sophistication about swingers today that did not exist twenty years ago and long may it continue. But one thing remains the same and that is the exhilaration, excitement and yes the danger. Swingers would not have it any other way.

CHAPTER 11

Zorro's Revenge

Danny's voice boomed at me down the phone, "Baz, you and Marie are still coming over this weekend, aren't you?"

"Yes, of course we are. All the arrangements are made. Don't worry," I answered. As usual. I was holding the receiver a couple of inches from my ear to keep the decibels within safety limits.

"Good, good. I was ringing to see if it's ok to invite another couple."

"No problem. The more the merrier. Who are they?" I asked.

"Oh, it's a couple we've been writing to for a bit. They're dead genuine and she's an absolute stunner. It's just that," he hesitated.

"Just what?" I asked beginning to hear alarm bells ringing. Danny's voice dropped to an uncharacteristic whisper.

"It's just that she's deaf."

"What's that? Did you say she's daft?"

"No, no, I said deaf, she's deaf," screamed Danny. "But like I say she's gorgeous and well up for it."

"Ok, I'm convinced," I said. "We'll see you Saturday."

"Oh, one more thing before you go," said Danny. "Ask Marie to wear those little frilly pink undies will you?"

"Sure will," I answered. "And see if Sue will wear the leather peep hole bra and those panties with the zip in the front."

"Got it. See you Saturday."

I put the phone down, still feeling a bit suspicious. Danny was not above playing the odd prank or two. He had once sent us a letter supposedly from a well-known lady newsreader that stated she was really into swinging and had seen an ad of ours and would we like to get together. If so, would we ring her office at the BBC to arrange a meeting? We had sussed that one easily enough, even though the letter had been immaculately written, on expensive bonded paper. The envelope bore a Doncaster postmark, which of course is where Danny and Sue live, and I didn't think too many BBC newsreaders commuted from Doncaster to London everyday.

Another time, we were all due to attend a house party in Hull. Danny had phoned to say the people holding the party had made it fancy dress. We duly arrived dressed as Zorro and Little Miss Muffett, only to find the other ten couples in normal clothes and Danny doubled up with laughter at the back of the room. The clothes soon came off and we all had a chuckle.

Later in the night I told Danny that we would take our revenge.

"No chance, Baz, you'll never catch us," he said

confidently. "And even if you do, the sight of you bursting through the door dressed as Zorro and swishing you're little plastic sword will be worth it. Laugh, I thought my trousers would never dry."

"I'll get you one day, don't you worry about that mate" I told him, but now here we were again. Was Danny setting us up or was the lady in question really deaf? If so, the only problem would be communication, but it wouldn't affect the end result.

So Saturday evening we set off along the M18, wondering what awaited us. Marie had threatened to do unspeakable things to Danny if this was another one of his pranks and had brought along her specially made suede whip to administer punishment should it be needed.

Sue's mum had taken their kids for the night, so it was a stay over. We always enjoyed our times with Danny and Sue. We were all so much alike in our thinking and lifestyles, and the sex with them was getting better every time we met. Marie and Sue were both bi and Danny and I loved to watch them make out. Even Danny's pranks added a hint of uncertainty to our adventures. It was a fun time for us all, and life was good.

Dusk was falling as we pulled up outside the neat little semi on the outskirts of Doncaster and, with our well worn overnight bag hanging from my shoulder, we walked up the flagstone garden path, past the rows of carefully tendered shrubs and flowers. The door opened before we had the time to knock, Sue stood in the hallway wearing a long black dress.

"Come in and close the door," she said. I shut the door behind me and turned to find that Sue had stepped out of her dress and was now standing provocatively in her leather peep-hole bra and panties with the zip open, revealing a profusion of dark pubic hair.

"Oh Suzy Q, look at you," I said as I pulled her to me for a kiss.

"You like sir?" she purred.

"I like," I answered standing back to admire the view again.

"Tart," exclaimed Marie as she hugged Sue. "You'll do anything to get a man. And speaking of men, where is he?"

"He's in the lounge, reading," said Sue.

"Reading?" said Marie, "Has he suddenly found culture?"

"Hardly," replied Sue, "He's studying."

"This I have to see," said Marie and off she shot into the lounge, leaving Sue and I to have another snog and a grope before following her.

In the lounge Danny was holding his hands up, with his fingers curled into what looked like a teapot.

"And this one means, do you like oral?" he told Marie who was desperately trying not to laugh. He then locked both hands together, consulted his book and made a rocking motion. "This one is, do you fuck?" Marie was making little squeaky noises and, Danny's seriousness only made the scene more comical.

After consulting his little book again, he opened his mouth and made a gulping motion, while simultaneously rubbing his stomach. "This one is saying, do you swallow? I think." He bent down again to consult his book of sign language.

A huge blast of laugher signaled that Marie had lost

her Herculean battle with the laughter monster. With tears streaming down her face, she fled to the kitchen with Sue to compose herself. "What's wrong with Marie?" asked Danny, seemingly hurt by her outburst of laughter.

"What happened to, hello, how are you?" I asked.

"Eh? Oh yeh. I was coming to that," said Danny. "Got to get the priorities right though, eh," he grinned.

"So there really is a deaf woman then?" I said.

"Of course there is, and she's a fucking stunner, mate. You'll come in your pants when you see her. That's why I've been out today and bought this book, I'm not going to lose the chance of shagging her because of poor communication. Here, what do you think this means?" Danny twisted his fingers into a configuration that looked painful and grimaced as he tried to hold it. "What's that mean?" he repeated.

"Tell me please, I can't stand the suspense," I answered. "Well, loosely translated it means you have great tits," he said triumphantly.

"You smooth talking bastard," I said. "How could any deaf woman resist you'?"

Danny still had his fingers twisted in a confused tangle when Sue and Marie came back into the lounge. Marie took one look at Danny's latest effort at learning sign language and fled back into the kitchen, screeching with laughter again. It was at least fifteen minutes before she could come back into the room without bursting into uncontrollable giggling fits.

Danny was defiant, "You can all laugh," he said. "But I will be the only one able to communicate with her tonight."

"I can just imagine the conversation," said Marie. "She'll say, 'Hello, how are you?' And you'll say 'You have great tits. Would you like to fuck? And do you swallow?"

"That should do it," I said. "If she isn't completely bowled over by your conversational skills, she must be a moron."

We all laughed, even Danny had to smile. "We shall see," he said. "We shall see."

A knock on the door brought Danny springing to his feet. "Fuck me it's them," he shouted, Sue had slipped back into her dress.

"Don't panic," she said. "I'll let them in." Danny was pacing the floor and remembered to push his little book down the side of a chair cushion just before Sue came back in, followed by the most gorgeous woman I had ever seen. She was about five feet six, with long, glistening, auburn hair that dropped to her waist. She wore a short, lilac-coloured dress that hugged her hour glass figure. Her face was straight off a Pirelli calendar. I could see now why Danny had made such a fuss. Her husband was tall and slim, with boyish good looks. A single curl hung onto his forehead from an otherwise immaculate haircut. I could see Marie and Sue giving him the once over.

"This is Barry and Marie," said Sue. "And Danny who you know from our letters. This is Alison and Andrew everyone." We all shook hands.

"Please call me Andy, everyone does," he said. "I suppose Sue and Danny have told you Alison is deaf?"

"Yes, they have mentioned it," I said." She does wear a hearing aid which helps a little, but she's an excellent lip-reader, so as long as you face her she will be able to understand."

"Great," said Marie. She went over to Alison and pronounced as clearly as she could. "Hi, my name is Marie, and this is my husband Barry." Alison responded by giving us both a kiss. I could see Danny in the background looking despondent. His long hours of study had been in vain. Sue opened a bottle of white wine and we sat around talking and learning more about our new, good-looking friends.

They were both in their late twenties and had only been swinging for a matter of months, and had experienced some great times. "You've not met a couple called Kenny and June then?" I asked.

"No are they friends of yours?" asked Andy. This brought a laugh and we warned them to stay clear of the Kenny and Junes of this world.

As the night went on I could see Alison giving me more than my fair share of eye contact. Eventually she came over and sat next to me on the sofa, resting her hand on my leg. I could see Danny casting envious glances my way. He would no doubt get his chance with this beauty at some stage in the evening, but both of us wanted to be first, so as Alison began to rub the inside of my thigh I felt confident that I had become first on the starting grid.

But Danny was not beaten yet. Even though his dubious sign language skills had been undermined by Alison's ability to lip read, he was determined to give it a try. After all it was his last and best hope of persuading Alison to grant him pole position.

Sue had put some smoochy tapes on the stereo and

the atmosphere was becoming sexually charged. Alison was on the brink of snogging me when Danny made his move. He came over and knelt in front of Alison. "I have a surprise for you," he said making over-exaggerated mouth movements.

"What is it?" Alison mouthed in reply.

My immediate reaction was to think 'Danny you shit. just as we were getting in to it.' But then I had this lovely warm feeling that if I gave Danny enough rope he would hang himself, so I sat back, folded my arms and let him get on with it.

He shuffled about on his knees until he was comfortable, "I want to tell you something in sign language," he said. Alison looked impressed, she smiled and nodded her approval. Danny consulted his book for a few seconds then screwed his face into a grimace in a desperate attempt to consign what he had seen to memory. Then he lifted his hands in readiness, but before he began he cleared his throat, which brought a giggle from Marie. Everyone watched as Danny began his routine, twisting and interlocking his fingers and waving his hands. It looked impressive and Danny's confident air made me wonder if he had actually pulled it off.

Alison sat impassively throughout and when it was over turned to Andy with a bemused look on her face. I suddenly had the lovely warm feeling again. "What did he say, Andy?" I asked eagerly.

"Well, it was a little difficult to follow," said Andy. "But as far as I can make out he said, welcome to my sheep on the mountain." Both Marie and Sue exploded into howls of laughter.

"No, no," exclaimed Danny. "I said welcome to my house."

"How did the mountain get in there'?" shrieked Marie in between bouts of laughter.

"Sod the mountain," I laughed. "I want to know about the sheep."

"Yes," said Sue. "I didn't know we had any sheep."

"Of course you do, Sue," I said. "It's the one you keep on the mountain."

"It's a mountain sheep," screamed Marie. She and Sue were now hugging each other in fits of laughter.

"You mean mountain goat," laughed Andy.

"No, I mean, Danny's not beyond mounting a few sheep if he has to," squealed Marie.

The room was in uproar. Danny was now crawling along the floor on his hands and knees, muttering that at least he had got the first word right. His ultimate weapon had backfired, exploded in his face, and shot him in the foot, all at the same time. But just as I began to wallow in my smug satisfaction Alison got up, went over to Danny and gave him a big kiss. "Thank you," she mouthed. Danny smiled over at me. The bastard I thought, he's done it on the sympathy card after all, but then Alison came back over, pulled me to my feet and we began to dance. The smoochies were still on and, with her head buried in my neck and her hands up my back and under my shirt, we slowly rotated to George Michael's, Careless Whisper. As I came round, I saw Danny toss his little book over the back of a chair. As he saw my smiling face resting on Alison's shoulder he mouthed something at me and I didn't need a book to understand him, I was indeed a jammy bastard.

With the battle to be first with Alison won, I began to relax and enjoy the feel of her in my arms. George Michael had finished and Elton John was half way through telling us why they called it the blues, when I decided to sneak upstairs with Alison. But as we left the room Danny shouted, "Hey, where are you two off to?"

"Alison has a headache. She needs to lie down," I quipped, which was greeted by a loud jeer.

"With you on top of her, I suppose," added Marie.

"Trust me, I'm a doctor," I said as we disappeared up the stairs.

I headed for the spare room, which I knew only had a single bed in it, but I wanted to be alone with Alison and I guessed that the rest of them would go to Danny and Sue's room, which was much bigger and of course had a double bed. I was still thinking logically, but I knew my male logic would desert me once I was alone with Alison, so my planning had to be done now, while I was still able to think coherently.

Once inside the small spare bedroom, I closed the door and turned on the bedside lamp. "Alone at last," I said. Alison took a step back and began to peel off her skin-tight, lilac dress. Slowly and provocatively she pulled the dress over her head and let it drop to the floor. Only then could I see her voluptuous figure in all its glory.

She unhooked her bra and let it fall, revealing perfectly formed breasts with protruding pink nipples. Her panties were the next to go. She was shaven. I had to stop myself from grabbing her, and throwing her onto the bed, but I wanted to savour the experience, make it last and enjoy every second. So I took hold of her hand

and gently led her to the bed where we began to kiss.

Now people kiss in a variety of ways. Some kiss with the mouth closed, some with the mouth open. Some like plenty of tongue action, some work the lips more, others prefer short sharp kisses, while some go for the long sloppy ones.

I have always found kissing to be a tremendous turn on for most women and always try to adapt to the style of kiss the woman I'm with has, it can be very awkward if a man and woman have vastly different styles of kissing. One has to adapt to the other, but Alison threw me totally. She not only kept her lips shut but made no movement whatsoever. Ok I thought. She doesn't like animated kisses. A few women don't. No problem, I'll try a long slow one instead. Still nothing. Right, I'll try inserting the tip of my tongue between her lips. That usually gets a reaction, but she just lay there motionless. I was kissing her neck, her chin, her lips, nothing, no movement at all. She looked like a Greek goddess but behaved more like a Greek statue.

So, she's not into kissing. Maybe it's just not her thing. Ok then, I'll work on her body. I slid down onto her breasts and began to nibble and suck her nipples. From one to the other I went, licking and sucking, tugging gently with my teeth and caressing with my hands. Alison still showed no reaction whatsoever.

Before we had got onto the bed I had had a raging erection but now it was diminishing as fast as my ego. Suddenly a flash of brilliance flooded my mind. Perhaps Alison is one of those rare women that doesn't like foreplay. Yes that must be it. She can't tell me herself, so she's letting me know by not responding, of course that must be it. Right, straight on to the main course then.

I positioned myself between her legs, which I had to push apart, and was ready for insertion.

Alison still lay on her back, with her eyes closed and her arms by her side. It was only the fact that her eye lids moved occasionally that reassured me she was not dead. I looked down at my dick. He was retreating into my body.

"Oh no you don't," I said. "You've got a job to do my lad." I thrust what was left of my erection into her, still nothing. I began frenziedly pumping in and out, trying to resurrect my hard-on, trying to get a reaction, trying not to let the rising tide of self doubt overwhelm me.

Faster and faster I pumped but she was totally unresponsive. I began to panic. Surely she must show some kind of emotion soon, a moan, a groan, anything would do.

Then suddenly I heard a squeak. Alison had responded. I was ecstatic. All my efforts had been worthwhile. She had squeaked. But hold on, could it have been a bedspring. I wasn't sure. I pumped hard some more and there it was again, a fucking bedspring. Oh shit, all that effort and it's a bedspring. Right, you bitch, you're going to get the full repertoire of my sexual know how, I thought. And if that doesn't make you squeal nothing will.

I tried the rotating hip thrust, the clit grind, the gyrating pit plunge, and the revolving pelvic pump, nothing worked. She just lay there, stone like. I had failed. She obviously found me a complete and utter turn off. In desperation I began nibbling her ear, in truth I couldn't think of what else to do.

Suddenly a loud high, pitch screeching split the air....
Wheeeeeeeeooooooowwweeeee! I was deafened and fell
back off the bed. Alison's hearing aid had reacted to my
breathing next to her ear and the feedback had been loud
enough to blast me back and leave my own ears ringing.
Alison at last opened her eyes and looked at me lying on
the floor. "Are you ok?" she mouthed.

"Yes," I answered. "I have to go to the toilet." I was
beaten. I had given my all, but it wasn't enough. I left the
room feeling totally dejected.

The rest of the gang were just coming up the stairs.
Danny shouted, "Didn't take you long mate. You must
have shot your load as soon as Alison looked at you." I
forced a smile and skulked off down the hall to the toilet.

As I reached the door Andy pulled me to one side,
"How did you get on with Alison?" he asked.

"She's, err, a gorgeous lady," I answered.

"She certainly is," replied Andy.

"But she's not very demonstrative. She drives me
crazy because she's so laid back when we make love. She
always says she's had a great time but I just wish she
would show it, but it's just her way I suppose. Still so
long as you've had a good time."

"Oh yeah, had a great time, thanks."

Marie came out of the main bedroom and took hold
of Andy's arm, "You're coming with me," she
whispered. "Duty calls," said Andy.

"I think Sue is waiting for you in here, Barry," added
Marie as she disappeared into the bedroom.

"I won't be a minute," I answered. The seeds of an
evil plan were growing in my mind. Danny was on his

way to Alison in the spare room when I called him over. He was rubbing his hands in anticipation.

"How was she, Baz?" he asked eagerly.

"She's a crazy woman mate, an absolute raver," I said. "Talk about throwing it around. You'll need a bloody saddle to ride her, Danny boy."

Danny clenched his fist and punched the air. "Yes, yes, I fucking knew it. I knew she'd be a wild one."

"Wild is not in it, mate. I'm telling you, if you can't get her going you've lost it. I've never seen anyone thrash around so much." By now Danny was hopping from one foot to the other with excitement.

"I had better get in there," he said. "Thanks for warming her up for me, Baz. Now its time for a real man to finish the job," he laughed.

As he got to the bedroom door I called to him again, "Danny."

"What?"

"Just one more thing. She loves to finish off with you blowing in her ear. It drives her fucking crazy." Danny gave me the thumbs up and disappeared into the bedroom.

Marie was already making it with Andy as I walked into the other room. Sue lay next to them, wearing her leather peep-hole bra and panties. The zip was already open. She looked at me with those big brown eyes and I had the lovely warm feeling again. God was in his heaven, Danny was with Alison, and all was well with the world. Sex with Sue was always great. We knew each other's likes and dislikes and could laugh together. That's important, and she was a hell of a lot better at it than Alison.

Marie and Andy were making lots of noise and rolling around the bed. But Sue and I managed to have a damn good session by climbing beneath the sheets and pulling them over our heads. Although Andy and Marie kept rolling on us, we still managed a tremendous sixty-nine that ended with a mutual orgasm.

Afterwards we all lay on the bed chatting and joking. Marie asked Andy what he did for a living, to which he replied, "I'm a banker."

Sue was in like lightning with, "Oh, don't be silly, we all love you."

We were still laughing when we heard it, a terrible screeching from the other bedroom.

Weeeeeeeeeeeeaaaaaoooooooweeee.

"What in heavens name was that?" exclaimed Sue. "Sounds like someone killing a cat," said Marie.

"No," said Andy. "It's feedback from Alison's hearing aid. Danny must be blowing in her ear. It makes a hideous, screeching sound. Alison won't hear it but it will scare the hell out of Danny I'll bet." Poor old Danny," I said, just managing to stifle a laugh.

It was around 2a.m. in the morning by the time everyone had reassembled down stairs and drinking the customary after-sex coffee. Andy and Alison were not staying over and, as we stood in the hallway saying our goodbyes, I caught Danny's eye and gave him the thumbs up. He forced a smile and half heartedly gave me a return gesture.

When Andy and Alison had gone we all returned to the lounge. I had briefed the girls on how I had set Danny up while he was making another coffee. The trap was set and I was determined to extract maximum pleasure from Danny's predicament.

"Well, Danny?" I said, as he returned carrying a tray of coffee cups.

"What?" he replied.

"Well, what did you think of Alison. What a ride, eh?"

Danny looked sheepish. "Yes, yes very good. How did you girls get on with Andy?" He was desperately trying to change the subject but I was like a dog with a bone.

"Never mind that," I said. "Did she wrap her legs around your waist and claw your back like she did with me?"

"Eh, oh, err yeh that, err. I can't believe I got the sign language wrong. I must have been looking at the wrong bit."

He was really beginning to squirm and the girls and I were enjoying every second. I pushed on, "I had a job keeping her on the bed, she was thrashing around so much. How did you manage it?" I asked eagerly.

"Oh, err, you know, just held on," he said with a nervous laugh. I decided to go for the throat.

"I'll tell you what, mate, any bloke that can't get her going should seriously think about taking a vow of celibacy. What do you say?"

"Oh, err, yeh. I should say so. Err, have I put sugar in this coffee?" he spluttered.

I wanted to continue the inquisition but Danny's last evasive answer had brought a shriek of laughter from the girls, so I told him the story on Alison. He slumped back into his chair and breathed a huge sigh of relief.

"Thank fuck," he announced. "I thought I'd lost it. I

was trying everything I knew. Nothing worked. It was like shagging a zombie and then I blew in her ear and fuck me that sound, I thought it was the end of the world. I take my hat off to you, Baz. You got me good and proper, so you did."

"Let's just call it Zorro's revenge," I said. Danny laughed and took a huge gulp of his coffee.

"You know, Baz, at one point I thought I'd got a reaction out of her when I heard a squeak."

"The bedspring?" I shouted.

"It fooled you too?" Danny said.

"Yes, yes," I answered. Danny threw back his head and roared with laughter. We laughed with him. All in all it had been a good night.

CHAPTER 12

Sightseeing in London

The first time I saw Marietta Concheeta Gonzales I couldn't work out if she was just a typical arm-waving, over-excitable, Latin woman or a complete, raving lunatic. She was holding centre stage in the basement of a wine bar in central London, which doubled as a venue for swingers at weekends. It was dimly lit and on the cold side.

The management had spread a few tables and chairs around and had set up a make-shift bar, and although the huge wooden barrels and cobweb-covered wine racks gave it an atmosphere of sorts, it could still best be described as the basement of a wine bar. It was full of the usual motley assortment of weirdo's, kinks, and normal people that the capital tended to attract to venues like this in the eighties.

We had travelled down by train on the Saturday and had booked in at a modest hotel on the Edgeware Road. Our plan was to have a night of debauchery at the club then, spend the Sunday sightseeing, before travelling home in the evening. But that was before we had met Marietta Gonzales. She was surrounded by about a dozen people who cheered and clapped as she rode a semi-naked man around the floor. The guy was complete with genuine riding saddle, stirrups, and mouth harness.

Marietta repeatedly lashed the poor guy's buttocks with a riding crop, making him scamper around the room. "Arriba Arriba," she shouted. As she dug her heels into his sides and brought the riding crop down for the umpteenth time upon his reddened backside. The crowd loved it, and as she passed our table I could see the glint of lust in her eyes. Eventually she pulled hard on the reins dragging the guy's head back and forcing him to stop. Slowly she stood up and pulled what looked like a sugar lump from her purse and fed it to her trusty steed, then without warning gave him a resounding whack with the crop. Off he galloped, presumably to be watered and fed back at the bar by some willing stable-hand.

Marietta threw her hat in the air, to a resounding cheer from her entourage and an ear-splitting yahoo from her. I pulled the sleeve of a single guy who seemed to be the tail-end Charlie of her following.

"Excuse me. Could you tell me who that woman is?" I asked. His look of disbelief that I did not know her prompted me into adding quickly, "We're not from around here."

That seemed to work, as the look of disbelief turned to a patronising smile. "She is Mistress Marietta Concheeta Gonzales, the best known dominatrix in London," he announced. The levels of illumination suddenly seemed to rise in the dark basement, or it could have been Marie's eyes, lighting up when she heard the word 'dominatrix'.

"She has her own fully fitted dungeon in Chelsea,"

he continued. "And the things she does to some of her slaves has to be seen to be believed."

He seemed to drift off down memory lane for a moment before Marie dragged him back to the present.

"A dungeon. She has her own dungeon?" she asked.

"Eh? Oh yes. Brilliant it is. I helped build some of the equipment, stocks and racks and stuff like that. She stretched me on the rack for an hour as payment" he said as the far away look returned to this face.

"You can come and put some shelves up at our house and I'll stretch you no problem," I laughed. Marie dug me in the ribs, but she needn't have bothered because Stretch was reminiscing so deeply again that he had not heard a word.

"We have got to introduce ourselves to her and see this dungeon," said Marie.

"That's easier said than done," I answered. "Look at her now." Marietta was sitting on the shoulders of another naked equestrian and had him running around, jumping over lengths of cane hung between two chairs. He wore the mouthpiece and reins, but instead of the riding crop she now had a short leather whip, which she used with some gusto and no little skill upon her steed's back and buttocks. He was a big, powerful-looking guy, but Marietta had him under complete control and soon had him jumping clear rounds.

Marie was standing on a chair for a better view as Marietta now had everyone in the club formed into an oval-shaped jumping arena. A huge 'Ole' greeted every successful jump and a collective groan followed the failed ones.

It was all great fun and I had to admit that this

outlandish Spanish lady had personality by the lorry-load. Suddenly Stretch was with us again, after somehow finding his way back from memory lane. "Isn't she fantastic? he said.

"She's great," Marie answered enthusiastically.

"A bunch of us will be going back to her place later. If you would like to come," he said. "I'm sure Mistress Marietta won't mind."

"That would be marvelous," Marie said. "I would love to see her dungeon."

"I'll have a word with her," said Stretch. "I'll see you later."

This worried me. I had known for some time that Marie wanted to learn more about the art of female domination, but I also knew that she was a woman of extremes. If she got drunk; she got staggering drunk. If she got mad; it was screaming hab-dabs kind of mad. If she was happy; it was all sweetness and light everything in the garden was rosy happy. There were no half measures, no grey areas. It was all or nothing. So once she had seen Marietta's dungeon she would want to go all the way. There would be no easing into it. She would jump in with both feet and end up hurting someone and that someone could be me.

I felt a tap on my shoulder and turned to see Stretch standing there with Marietta. "I would like to introduce Mistress Marietta Concheeta Gonzales," he said.

"I'm pleased to meet you," I answered feeling as though I was in the presence of a celebrity. "My name is Barry and this is my wife, Marie."

Marietta stood there half smiling, or not half smiling I wasn't sure. She was about thirty-six, slightly on the heavy side with big boobs and large thighs. Her waist, though, looked quite slim, mainly due to the red silk Basque she wore being laced extremely tight. It had the added benefit of pushing her already ample breasts upwards and outwards, to the point where they looked as though they were ready to explode. On her bottom half she wore soft leather chaps with the front and back totally exposed and only a tiny thong covering her pubic area. She was typically Spanish in looks, with shiny, black hair, full red, painted lips and large almond eyes. Attractive would be the wrong word to describe her. In fact, she made no attempt to be attractive, at least not in the classical sense. She was striking, that description suited her better, and I believe that is the image she cultivated.

"I am told you would like to see my dungeon," she said, addressing herself to Marie in a very abrupt and very Spanish accent.

"Yes. I would love to," said Marie.

"I live in Chelsea," said Marietta, still looking past me and at Marie. "I will be taking a group of people back with me later, if you would care to join us?"

"Yes, we'd love to," Marie answered.

Marietta looked a me for a moment, as though she was deciding if I was worthy enough to be in her presence or not, then in her husky, Latin voice exclaimed, "Yes, bring your man if you like. I'm sure you will both find it very interesting." She turned away for a moment, and then turned back to Marie.

"I will be penetrating a man later but I have not decided who yet. Have you ever seen a man penetrated?"

"No, I haven't," Marie answered.

"They squeal," said Marietta. "They like to ram their pathetic, male members into us, but when the roles are reversed, they can't take it. They squeal."

"Yes. I should think they would," replied Marie.

Marietta continued, "I will show you my chamber and later I will show you how to penetrate a man." She leaned over and kissed Marie on the lips and was gone, engulfed by her adoring fans once more.

"She's a nut case," I said. "Well she's not fucking penetrating me. No way is she coming anywhere near my fucking arse."

"Oh, don't be silly," Marie answered. "She doesn't mean you. Anyway it's probably all talk. We'll just go and see her dungeon, that's all."

"She's just a man hater, anyone can see that," I said. "Did you notice how she ignored me and just spoke to you? She'd penetrate me as soon as look at me that one."

"Nonsense," Marie retaliated. "She's a dominatrix, that's the way they are. All men are slaves to her, but she doesn't hate them. You're just being silly."

I wasn't convinced, but reluctantly agreed to go over to Chelsea and view Marietta's torture chamber. And my resolve to keep my buttocks well clenched was strengthened even more when I saw the way Marietta was now using what looked like a hand paddle on some poor sod's backside.

As the night wore on, I became more and more nervous at the prospect of visiting Marietta's dungeon, but I could see Marie was excited by it. I knew it was something she had desperately wanted to explore ever since the night at Blockley Manor when she had whipped the guy tethered to the post. The last thing I wanted was to hold her back, but then neither did I want to run the risk of being penetrated by a crazy, Spanish, man–hating dominatrix.

I was still lost in thought when a voice from the past rang in my ear. The sound of it sent a chill down my spine. "What are you two doing here?" I spun round to see the familiar sickly Cheshire cat grins of Kenny and June.

"Oh, it's you," I blurted out stating the obvious.

"Of course it's us," laughed Kenny. "Fancy seeing you here, you're a long way from home."

"Oh yes, we're down for the weekend," I stammered.

Marie was just returning from the toilet and must have thought I had met a new couple as Kenny and June had their backs to her.

"Hi there," she said breezily, as she came round. Suddenly the realisation of who she was talking to hit her and the look of shock and horror on her face made me cringe. But as usual it went way over the heads of Kenny and June.

"Hi ya, babe," said Kenny. "Oh those little titties of yours have got bigger." He made a lunge for Marie's breasts, but she expertly sidestepped him and sat down at the table.

Meanwhile June had sidled up to me, "I've missed that dick of yours," she whispered.

'I don't know why,' I thought. 'You only got half of it and you were lucky to get that.'

"Oh I should think you've had bigger cocks than mine," I replied.

"But it's how you use it," she said.

"You certainly used mine," I answered. Again the sarcasm missed her by a country mile. As her hand began to slide down my thigh I hastily sat down next to Marie. Kenny and June sat down opposite us, both still brandishing those inane grins.

"Well," said Kenny scanning the room. "Are their any new couples in tonight?"

"No, I don't think so," I answered. "Quite a few weirdos though." 'And we're sat with two of them,' I thought.

"So do you come here often?" asked Marie in a transparent attempt to avoid them in future.

"Three or four times a year," answered Kenny. "We always manage to find some action."

"What about that young couple we had last time?" interrupted June.

"Oh, yes," said Kenny. "Fresh out of school by the look of 'em. Took them back to our hotel and shagged them silly, didn't we babe?"

"You made her come double fast, didn't you Ken?" said June.

"Sure did. She was even faster than you, Marie, and I got you hot real quick. Didn't I doll?"

I could see Marie's face flush with anger. Any second now, I thought her flimsy self-restraint will evaporate and all hell will break loose.

Just then Stretch appeared at our table. "Mistress Marietta is leaving shortly if you would care to follow us."

"Yes, yes," said Marie. "We'll grab a taxi outside and follow you."

"Hey, hey," said Kenny. "What's all this? Holding

out on us, are you? What's happening?"

"Oh it's nothing, just going to view a dungeon," I said trying to play it down.

"A dungeon," said June. "Oh I would love to see that."

"It's ok if we tag along, isn't it?" said Kenny. "We can all share a taxi."

Before we had time to say anything, Stretch said that Marietta had invited anyone who cared to go.

My heart sank. Not only were we about to follow a crazy woman to who knows where, but we were also stuck with Kenny and June.

Our taxi was fifth in the cavalcade. It was about two in the morning but the streets of the capital were still buzzing with clubbers, tourists and the homeless. Down Shaftsbury Avenue, along Piccadilly and past the rows of Georgian mews houses, with their neat lines of ornate iron railings and eventually turning into a quiet side street off the Kings Road.

The convoy of taxis stretched half the length of the road as the lead cab pulled up outside a middle-of the row, three storey, terrace house. At least two dozen people alighted from the row of taxis and followed the caped figure of Marietta down a short flight of steps and through the large front door.

The long inner corridor was festooned with elaborately framed paintings of bullfights and brightly coloured matadors wearing red capes. The decor was either red or black, with the odd gold cornice thrown in. As we all trooped snake-like along the corridor, I couldn't help but wonder if this was all going to end in tears (mine).

Marietta swung left at the head of snake and the

entourage dutifully followed. There must have been around twenty-five people or so, but only about six or seven women as part of couples. All the rest were single males who acted like slaves to their Spanish goddess, seeing to her every need. One respectfully removed her cape, while another knelt down on his hands and knees behind her so she could use his back as a chair. The room maintained the colour scheme of red walls, black skirting and gold dado rails surrounding ornate wall lights. It was all quite regal and Marietta did not look out of place as the queen.

Once everyone was assembled in the room, Marietta lifted herself from her human chair and spoke.

"You are all welcome to my habitat and soon we shall visit my dungeon. For those of you who have not been before there is only one rule, the female must be obeyed. Every woman in this place has complete dominance and any male must do her bidding. If that is not acceptable then he should leave now. If you stay, you obey."

Marietta was flanked by three big guys, who were obviously there to enforce her rule. Two of the couples present decided to leave, one of the women really wanted to stay but her husband almost dragged her out in his haste to leave.

I looked at Marie in a vain attempt to persuade her to follow them. "Don't worry," she whispered. "I'll protect you."

"Oh shit," I thought. "I'm dead."

Kenny whispered in my ear. "Let them go, Barry. More fanny for us." The mandatory grin was still glued to his face.

'You thick twat,' I thought. 'This lot don't want to shag us, it's more likely we'll get whipped to a pulp and then penetrated.' At that moment I began to make plans to run for it should I need to, with Marie over my shoulder if necessary.

Marietta spoke again. "Very well. Now the unbelievers have left we can begin." She breezed past us back into the corridor and turned into a room at the far end. We all filed after her. It took a few minutes for our eyes to get used to the dark. This was Marietta's famed dungeon.

The room was large, about 30 feet square. It could have been two rooms knocked together. The colour scheme was reversed, with black walls and red edging. It was full of equipment of every description, some, more obvious than others. There were stocks, racks, cages, and a few dubious-looking contraptions that I couldn't work out. One of Marietta's minions was lighting four huge wax dribbled candles that stood in the corners of the rooms. The only other light in the dungeon were two dim wall lights on opposite walls. Gothic music began to play from some unseen stereo and smoke capsules were released, resulting in a haze that hung about a foot from the floor. I half expected Vincent Price to spring out from behind the stocks.

A few of the single guys were stripping off and being tied or shackled to various machines in readiness for Mistress Marietta to administer punishment. She was again seated on her human chair, awaiting the preparations to be completed. Once the naked men were tied in place Marietta stood up, walked over to the nearest one who was held in a pair of low stocks, which forced him to bend at the waist and leave his backside totally exposed. Marietta stood behind him, hands on hips. "Whip," she shouted and immediately one of her slaves ran up and reverently placed a long, black, leather whip in her hand. He then stuck a postage stamp onto one of the arse cheeks of the prone slave.

Marietta took three steps back and cracked the whip onto the man's arse, expertly dislodging the stamp and leaving a bright red mark in its place. She then moved one step forward and landed three resounding lashes onto his backside in quick succession. The man screamed in pain as Marietta continued to thrash him. She was not holding back. I could see she was putting all her considerable weight behind each stroke and she was soon perspiring heavily. I could also see the look in her eyes as she administered the beating. She was turned on big time. Her tongue continuously licked over her lips and her eyes widened and narrowed with each stroke.

As the slave's arse began to turn a dark purple she began to moan, softly at first, but with each stroke she became louder and more animated.

Marie gripped my arm and pulled me close so she could whisper in my ear. "My God, she's coming."

Marreeta suddenly threw the whip to one side. "Cane, cane," she gasped. A cane was quickly put into her outstretched hand. She swished it down hard onto the discoloured backside leaving a black line. The slave screamed, Marietta screamed. Again and again she brought the cane down, each time wailing in ecstasy until she reached a crescendo, when she stood shaking, with her eyes rolled up into her head and her knuckles whitened as she clenched the cane. Her arms went rigid and shook as she stood there, shuddering like someone who couldn't let go of a live cable. Her mouth was open in a silent scream.

Everyone in the room was spellbound. Then she suddenly let out the most guttural of sounds, "Ohhhhhhaaaaaaaa, ahhaaaaa," which ended in a short sharp "aha, aha, aha, aha, aha."

She then seemed to slump slowly forward, as the cane dropped from her limp hand. Two of her slaves rushed to catch her before she fell and helped her away to the back of the room, this time finding her, a real chair to sit in.

I turned to Marie, "Wow, what do you think of that?" I asked.

She didn't answer, instead she took my hand and put it down the front of her panties. She was soaking wet." Does that answer your question?" she said.

Before I had time to respond, Marietta's voice echoed around the room albeit weaker than before.

"Use the men," she shouted. "Use the men as you see fit, ladies."

'Oh shit, here we go,' I thought. Luckily, not counting Marietta, there were only five women in the room, and one of those was Marie, compared with over twenty men so at least the odds were on my side. I stuck close to Marie as though I was her slave. Mercifully June was off screwing someone who had caught her eye. Kenny was running around trying to get noticed. He still had not understood the situation. He was still under the impression that he could take any woman he wanted. Old habits die hard.

A couple of the women in the room were at a loss as

to what to do, but not Marie. She was looking for a spare whip to get a spot of practicing in. Many of the regular guys were already stripped off and were being strapped into or onto the pieces of equipment. It was obvious this is what they were into. It suited me fine as I was able to stand in the shadows, out of the way, and watch.

Things were beginning to get hairy. All the women were now becoming involved in different ways. Two of them were half heartedly whipping a couple of guys. Another was stretching a man on the rack but kept asking him if he was ok, which defeated the purpose, I thought. Marie had found a whip and to her credit was not just thrashing around aimlessly like the others but really trying to master the wrist action. I could see she was having a great time and, as long as I was safe in the shadows, I was quite happy to let her have her fun.

We had played a few times between ourselves but I'm not naturally submissive so it didn't really give her the chance to feel the complete female dominance that she craved and which made her so horny. Kenny was still desperately trying to get his end away, but the few women who were there were spoilt for choice, so he was getting nowhere fast. June was still doing the rounds with a succession of different guys.

After about thirty minutes or so, someone rang a gong and all the action stopped. Marietta seemed to have recovered from her monumental climax. "It is time," she announced. "It is time for me to penetrate a man." There was silence. No one moved. It was reminiscent of an auction when no one dare twitch for fear of buying something.

Then from the back of the room came Kenny, who

had been busy trying to persuade one of the ladies to have sex with him and had obviously only half heard Marietta's announcement.

"What's that about penetration?" he shouted. "I'm up for some of that." He bundled past me, pushing a couple of the single guys out of the way in his haste to get to Marietta. "Suckers," he shouted as he bounded to the centre of the room.

"So you will be the one?" said Marietta.

"You got it, babe. I'm your man," said Kenny confidently.

I looked across at Marie. She put a finger on her lips. I didn't need telling. There was no way I was going to put Kenny straight. This was a dream come true. If ever a man deserved to be on the receiving end of what he had been dishing out over the years, it was him.

June had moved to her fourth guy of the evening and was just as oblivious of Kenny's impending predicament as he was.

"Let's get this on, sweetheart. I don't mind an audience, in fact I work better with a crowd," Kenny bragged.

"Prepare him," ordered Marietta. Seconds later the three heavies had taken hold of Kenny's arms and bent him forward over a three-foot high padded bench, tying his wrists and ankles to steel rings attached to the bottom of the wooden legs.

"Hey guys, easy. I'm not going to accomplish much in this position now am I," said Kenny.

Suddenly Stretch appeared holding a rubber ball with two straps attached to it. It was a gag, and as it was pushed into Kenny's mouth and the straps tied tight around the back of this head, the horrified look in his eyes told me the realisation of what was happening had finally filtered through to his dimly lit oversexed brain. But it was too late. Marietta was already strapping on a huge, black, rubber dildo.

As Stretch dragged Kenny's trousers down to his ankles, Marie came over to me and squeezed my hand. "I told you it was a good idea coming here," she whispered.

"I'll never doubt you again," I whispered back.

Marietta was oiling the dildo, which I thought was a compassionate touch. Kenny's eyes were darting around the room looking for help and he was making frantic grunting sounds. Suddenly he froze and his eyes widened.

Marietta had placed the tip of the dildo into his arsehole. She then addressed the room, "This act of penetration is a symbol of the superiority of the female over the lowly male, and by this deed all males shall acknowledge my dominance." She then thrust the full length of the monstrous dildo into Kenny's backside.

A loud cheer went up as Kenny's head shot up to reveal two huge, bulging eyes. He let out a sort of muffled scream that sounded like gravel in a blending machine. "Now that has got to hurt," I said.

"Well, he could always fake an orgasm if he wants her to stop," answered Marie.

We looked at each other and burst into laughter. As Marietta slowly withdrew the dildo, Kenny's head dropped in relief, but his respite was only brief as she instantly plunged it back in again. This time there was no pause for effect.

Marietta was now pumping in and out of Kenny as fast as it was possible to go, given that the dildo was about nine inches long and she was making sure that he was getting the full benefit of every inch. His head was thrashing around wildly but I could see his eyes were now shut tight and trails of saliva were splashing from the corners of his gagged mouth. He wasn't screaming as much now, he seemed more intent on just surviving. If Marietta had been a man she would have been a Kenny. She was all pumping and no technique. A few short strokes now and again wouldn't have come amiss, I thought, just to vary the pace a little. I'm sure Kenny would have agreed with me if he could have had a say.

But no, Marietta just kept slamming into his arsehole. It was ghastly and shocking, and it was sweet revenge.

Eventually Marietta ceased pumping and slowly pulled the giant dildo out of Kenny's rigid body. As she stood back Kenny gave a final rasping grunt and his body sort of flopped and hung there on the padded bench. "Christ, she's killed him," I said.

"No, no, look he's moving," said Marie. Kenny slowly lifted his head and opened his tear filled eyes. Just then June burst through the crowd.

"Kenny, Kenny, what have they done to you?" She ran up to him, inserted her finger and thumb into the corners of his mouth and pulled out the rubber ball gag. Unfortunately she did not unfasten it at the back of his head and it slipped from her fingers and smacked Kenny in the face.

"Ooooo, right in the kisser. He could have done without that," I winced.

"Get me out of here, babe. I think that bitch has damaged me," croaked Kenny. June set about freeing him, as the rest of the crowd began to melt away.

Marietta had already departed, followed by her entourage. Kenny stood up very slowly.

"Oooohh, aahhhh, oohhh," he whimpered, as June gingerly pulled up his trousers. Kenny began taking little baby steps as he hung on June's shoulder and crossed the room.

Suddenly he stopped, "Hold on babe," he said. "I've got to stop for a bit."

"What's wrong?" asked June."

"Nothing, just don't move. I have to stand still." Kenny screwed up his face and went rigid. "Oooohhh, no, oh... Please.., no... Aaaahhhh... oohhhhh."

"Kenny, what's the matter?" said June.

"I... think... I've... shit... myself," he sobbed.

"Oh my poor baby," cried June. "What have they done to my Kenny?"

We watched as they shuffled out of the dungeon and down the hallway to the front door. We felt a kind of grim satisfaction. Kenny and June had set out that night to gain maximum pleasure at the expense of others, just as they had done a hundred times before, but this time the tables had been well and truly turned. We couldn't feel sympathy for them. After all they had almost destroyed us the first time we had met, and we were only one of many couples to suffer at their hands. Not that Kenny's night of terror changed their behaviour, as over the years we have heard that they are still up to their old tricks. Although one report from a couple who had met them in the late eighties made us smile. They told us that Kenny suffered from poor bowel control, and had to keep dashing off to the loo. When we told them how he got that way we all had a good laugh.

As for Marietta, she went on to become something of a legend in the London bondage scene, finally returning home to her beloved Spain in the early nineties to continue her quest for female domination in the clubs and cellars of Madrid.

We left Marietta's and walked down to the embankment through a soft September morning twilight and caught a taxi back to our hotel.

We slept through most of the next day until it was time to catch our train home, so we missed our planned sightseeing tour, but we took the view that we had seen enough sights for one day.

CHAPTER 13

Dunroamin

As Christmas of 1984 approached, our search for a place where we could meet people close to home became a priority. We were tired of travelling hundreds of miles for swinging sessions, and we had decided not to bring couples back to our home while the kids were there. We had lost count of the number of times we had gone to see couples at their homes, only to be asked to keep the noise down as the kids were asleep in the next bedroom, or be told we couldn't go upstairs because the kids were still awake. The settee became all-important in those situations, as it's the most comfortable place to have sex downstairs in most homes.

So it ends up as a sort of musical chairs scenario, where one lucky couple manages to commandeer the sofa and the other couple has to make do with a single chair or more commonly the floor. I've had sex on cold, hard kitchen floors, hallways, breakfast bars, kitchen worktops, in utility rooms, and numerous lounge floors, and all because the kids were upstairs. It was always hugely off putting to be told that little Jimmy was still awake upstairs, so could we please not moan or shout when we climaxed.

Another massive turn off, even when the kids had been farmed out for the evening, was being taken to a child's bedroom to make out. When couples want to go to separate rooms, either Marie or I would end up in the kid's bedroom. I always dreaded this. There is nothing worse than trying to feel horny and make love to a woman when you are surrounded by toys and colouring crayons etc. and, worst of all, actually making love on the child's bed, knowing that they will be sleeping there the following night. It never failed to astound me how many parents can happily screw in their own children's bedroom, without feeling in the least bit inhibited.

I have struggled to perform many times in such circumstances, and on occasion failed completely to manage an erection. This usually depended on how much of it you could block out of your mind, but the smallest thing could ruin your concentration. I remember being with a woman in her daughter's bedroom and managing to keep single minded enough to perform, but at a crucial moment I happened to glance sideways and see a child's painting stuck on the wall. It was enough to shatter my fragile composure and I lost my erection completely. The lady in question could not understand the problem and was not happy that I requested that we go down to the living room to finish off. The whole thing got so bad that we began turning down couples when we knew there would be the kids in the house, or separate rooms were involved.

It all came to a dreadful conclusion one night in Lichfield, when we had, as usual, been told by the couple that, because the kids were asleep upstairs, we would have to stay in the living room. "Here we go again," I thought, and for once I managed to secure the settee with the lady of the house, leaving Marie and the guy to make the best of it on the carpet.

We had been going for about fifteen minutes or so and I had just changed positions, from missionary to doggy. when the living room door slowly opened and in walked a young girl of about six or seven. She wore a long pink nightie and held an empty glass in her hand. "Can I have a drink of water, mummy?" she said, as she stood in the doorway watching us. I froze and glanced at Marie who was, at least, mostly covered by the guy who was on top of her. We were all naked and I can't even begin to imagine what the youngster must have thought, seeing her mother and father totally naked with two complete strangers. It seemed to last for an eternity before the mother calmly said, "Go back upstairs to your room, sweetheart, and I'll bring you one up." The young girl turned and went back upstairs without saying a word or showing any emotion.

I fell back, with my head in my hands.

"Oh, Christ," I said. "Oh Jesus Christ almighty."

Marie meanwhile had literally thrown the guy off her and was frantically putting her clothes back on. The couple in question seemed unfazed and did their best to make light of it, telling us that their daughter regularly sleepwalked and would most likely not remember a thing in the morning. After which the glass of water was taken up and they wanted to carry on where we had left off.

By that time, we were fully dressed and just wanted to go home. Sex was the last thing on our minds, but the couple still did their best to persuade us to stay.

On the drive home that cold December night in 1984, we decided we would look for a little bolt hole close to home. This would serve a dual purpose. Firstly, it would enable us to meet people without their kids being around, and secondly it saved us the hassle and expense of travelling all the time. That is why we now stood in the late afternoon drizzle, looking up at the one-bedroom flat above a small post office, in a quiet suburb of Sheffield. The entrance was via a stairway from a yard at the back, where there was parking for two cars, perfect.

We were met, at the top of the stairs, by a wizened looking gentleman who looked to be about two hundred years old, we followed him at a snail's pace from room to room. as he told us in minute detail everything that had been done to the flat over the last fifty years. "And in 1975 we had a new boiler installed," he wheezed. "Then in 1976, no wait, I tell a lie, it was 1977. Yes, that's right, 1977 we had a new door fitted to the bedroom. And do you know how long that bath has been in?" he said with a knowing smile. "Forty years, that's how long. They don't make them like that anymore."

"Would you mind if we put in a shower over the bath," asked Marie.

The old man glared at us and one eye narrowed down to a crack. "It wouldn't cost me anything?" he asked.

"No, no of course not. We would pay for it to be installed and it wouldn't damage the bath," answered Marie.

He glared some more, "Hmmmm, if you must," he said grudgingly. "I don't hold with showers though, you can't beat a good hot bath." He went on, "Soaks all the grime out of the skin. Many's the time I've laid in that bath, and you could fair see the grime coming out of my skin. Settles on the top of the water it does, you don't get that with showers. They don't touch the grime. No you can't beat a good steaming hot bath, don't hold with showers, never have."

"Remind me to buy a bath mat," Marie whispered.

It took another twenty minutes for our ancient tour-guide to take us around the one bedroom flat. Finally we arrived back at the front door. "If you want it the rent is seven pounds a week, plus bills. With one month in advance," said the old man.

"We'll take it," I said. "We'll bring you the money tomorrow and pick the keys up."

As we followed our new landlord down the stairway and into the backyard, he turned to us and asked, "Will you be living here?"

"Err, no," I answered. "I'm a writer you see and I, err, need somewhere quiet to write."

"A writer," he gasped, the knowing smile returning to his face. "Only ever knew one writer years ago, bent as a nine bob note he was."

The old man was still shaking his head and muttering to himself as he climbed into his rusty old Ford Anglia. It was obvious he didn't hold with writers.

"Quick thinking that," Marie said. "My husband, the writer."

"Well, it seemed better than telling him we wanted to turn his flat into a den of debauchery," I said.

"But it's not a bad idea, is it?" Marie said.

"What, turning his flat into a den of debauchery?"

"No, I mean writing. You could write a book about

the things we've seen and done these last few years."

"Do you thing the world is ready for it?" I said.

"Maybe not," she said. "But it would be one heck of a book."

"One day," I said. "I'll write it one day."

The following week we set to work preparing our new little hidey hole in readiness for our first secret assignation. The flat itself was quite small, with just one bedroom, living room, bathroom and tiny kitchen. It was mostly unfurnished with just the carpets and the odd chair left. We went to a local factory outlet and picked up a damaged pull-out bed settee for half price. The spring had gone on one side, so it took two people to drag it out into a bed, but we didn't care about that. It would serve its purpose. We also picked up a cheap double bed with a mattress the depth of a wafer, and Marie made up some net curtains for the windows. The following week, I got a plumber to fit a shower over the antique bath and we finished off by digging some cups and an old electric kettle out of the back of the cupboards at home and picking up some new bedding from the local market. A final lick of white paint around the place added the finishing touch. It had been an exciting time for us. We were like a couple of kids in our enthusiasm for Dunroamin, as we had jokingly nicknamed our new retreat. So by January 1985 we were ready to add the words 'travel or accommodate' on to the end of our adverts, but just when it seemed everything was going great life threw a huge spanner in the works

The New Year began with bad news; Danny had been involved in a bad traffic accident and was in intensive care. It had been his first day back at work after the Christmas and New Year holiday. Danny had been driving the van full of insulation equipment to the first job when an articulated lorry coming towards him had jack-knifed and slammed into his van, knocking it off the road and into a field. It seems to have somersaulted a couple of times, before coming to rest on its side. It had happened that morning and Sue had been at the hospital all day.

It was now 8:30 in the evening and Sue had just arrived home to see the kids and grab a bite to eat before returning to the hospital. She seemed to be holding together as she spoke on the phone to Marie.

"They think it was ice on the road," said Sue.

"We'll come over straight away and take you to the hospital," said Marie.

"No, they won't let you in. It's just close family," answered Sue.

"Then we'll wait outside."

"No, honestly. I'm ok. My mum's here with the kids and my dad will run me to the hospital. There's really nothing you can do," Sue said. "I just had to ring to let you know what had happened."

I took the phone from Marie. "Sue, its Barry. How badly injured is he?" I asked, immediately castigating myself for being so blunt.

"They aren't sure just yet. He's got a broken leg and a broken arm. He's been unconscious since they brought him in. He could have head injuries, they don't know yet. They have to do some tests. He could have internal injuries too. I'll know more when I get back." A noticeable tremor in her voice betrayed the strain she was under.

Sue, I know we would just be in the way right now, if we came over, and you're right there's nothing we can do, but I want you to remember that we're here for you anytime at all. If you need anything, just call and we'll be there." I know, Barry, and thanks. I'll call when I have some news."

I put down the phone and sat next to Marie on the sofa. Neither of us spoke, we were both numb. Finally Marie stood up. "I'll put the kettle on," she said.

"Plenty of sugar in mine," I said. We both walked into the kitchen. "I think I'll get some fresh air," I said and walked on to the back garden. It was a cold, brittle night with the beginnings of a frost edging the grass, making it crunch under foot. Smoke from a neighbour's garden fire drifted across the lawn. In the distance I could hear voices, teenagers laughing and joking, having fun, that apart the night was quiet and still, with a bright, sharp moonlight.

Four years ago I had stood on this very spot, in the middle of a raging storm, holding onto Marie, holding onto our future. Four years ago we had won our fight for survival. Now Danny had to win his. My friend, our friend was lying close to death and I could do nothing to help him. This man was as close to me as a brother. We had shared good times and bad, shared our hopes and dreams and deepest emotions, shared our wives.

Once when Marie and Sue were out shopping, Danny and I had gone to the pub and in our drunken state had sworn to look after the other's family should one of us die. Now, as I stood in the hard cold of that January evening watching my breath freeze into the night. I began to ponder the practicalities of keeping my promise. "Tea's ready." Marie shouted from the back door.

"Ok," I answered. As I walked back I told myself, "He's not dead yet, Baz. So don't write the big paddy off too soon."

Back in the kitchen Marie and I hugged, don't worry," I said. "He'll be ok; he's too stubborn to die."

"I know," she answered. "But what rotten luck, and what must Sue and the kids be going through."

"Whatever happens they'll get through it. We'll see to that," I said.

We didn't get much sleep that night. I kept hearing Danny's booming voice and seeing him in half dreams, his black, curly hair forever falling over his face, the infectious laugh, the almost naïve sense of adventure, and the heart as big as a house. The night was a long one, and the temptation to ring Sue early the next morning was resisted, only because we feared it would be an intrusion and Sue would most likely be at the hospital anyway. By dinnertime we could wait no longer. Marie rang the hospital to be told that, because we were not close family, they could not disclose any details of Danny's conditions. An hour later, I was on the phone telling them I was Danny's brother. After a short silence I was told that Danny had gone to theatre that morning because of internal injuries, and he was due back in intensive care anytime now. If I rang back later they should know more.

The lead up to Christmas and New Year had been an exciting time for us. Putting the finishing touches to our new flat had been fun, and we had planned to have Danny and Sue over to christen Dunroamin in mid

January. Now our euphoria had turned into despair and Dunroamin would stand unused and collecting dust for months to come. Danny's accident had, had a galvanising effect on us. Tragedy in any friendship transcends all other feelings and swingers are no different. Our over riding priorities now were to help Danny and Sue in any way we could. We put all other couples on hold and forgot about Dunroamin.

Sue rang that night to say Danny had had surgery that day and although still seriously ill, was out of danger. She sounded relieved but was plainly shattered and almost out on her feet. Before she put the phone down, she told us the full catalogue of Danny's injuries. He had broken his right arm, right leg and collarbone. He also had a ruptured spleen, five cracked ribs and numerous cuts and bruises. The good news was that there was no sign of head injuries and, all being well, he would in time make a full recovery. Sue told us we could visit as soon as he was out of intensive care and back on a normal ward.

"A strange thing happened though," said Sue. "One of the nurses told me Danny's brother had rung to see how he was but I can't work out how he knew. He lives in America and I haven't been able to reach him yet."

"Must be psychic," I said. "Anyway, you get some sleep now, Sue. We'll speak again tomorrow." I put down the phone, thinking that at least I could have put on an Irish accent when I had rung the hospital.

Two weeks later we were walking up the wide road leading to Doncaster Royal Infirmary. Danny had been moved to a side ward the day before, and now, armed with grapes, magazines and a selection of tapes for his walkman, we were allowed our first visit.

There were three other beds in the sideward, two of them empty and one with an old guy, who just sort of lay there staring. Danny's right leg was encased in plaster up to the hip. A large pulley and weight system attached to the end of his bed supplied the traction. There was also a plaster cast on his right arm that overlapped onto his upper chest and finished somewhere around his back. There was also a moulded plastic brace clamped around Danny's neck, and various tubes and drains running in and out of his body. All in all he looked terrible. Sue and Marie were fussing around him plumping his pillows, straightening his sheets, and generally acting like mother hens.

"How's it going, mate, or is that a silly question?" I asked.

"Oh, I'm ok, Baz," croaked Danny. "I just feel so bloody stupid lying here. I can't even get up for a pee."

"Oh yeah. Sorry to hear about your wedding tackle," I said.

"What are you on about?" Danny asked.

"You don't know, then?" I continued.

"I don't know what?" he asked.

"Your balls were caught in the door when you crashed. They're in a field somewhere up near the Ml8."

Danny's good hand shot down under the blankets, his eyes widened as he felt around under the sheets and then a smile spread across his face. "He, he, you bugger, I'll get my own back when I'm better," he said.

"I know you will, mate, that's why I'm ragging you now, while you're weak and helpless."

"Here, you see that old fella in the bed opposite," Danny said.

"Yes," I answered.

"Well, all he does is stare you know. He gives me the ebi gebies so he does." I looked over and sure enough the old man just lay there staring.

"Are you sure he's not dead?" I said.

"Well, if he isn't now, he soon will be. I'm going to smother him tonight." Danny tried to laugh but only succeeded in hurting his ribs.

"Here we'll have none of that," I said. "You'll make yourself ill. Give me that pillow and I'll do it for you." Sue said it was the first time she'd seen Danny laugh since the accident.

Over the next four weeks we had Sue and the kids over to our house on numerous occasions. I even took Danny's 10-year-old son, Liam, to Bramall Lane, home of Sheffield United, in the hope of teaching him the finer points of football. In retrospect, it was probably not the best place to take a young lad to teach him that particular aspect of the beautiful game.

Bit by bit Danny recovered, but not without setbacks. His leg, which had been broken in two places below the knee, was not healing properly. One of the fractures was refusing to knit together, so Danny had to undergo another operation, called a sliding bone graft, in order for it to heal. If the operation had not worked then he would have faced the prospect of having his leg amputated. It was another harrowing time for Danny and Sue. Luckily all went well, and Danny's leg began to mend as it should, although it did mean an extra month in hospital, which did not appeal to him at all.

By April Danny was home for good and convalescing. He still had a full leg plaster on but, his arm was now only supported by a heavy bandage. Sue now became the main concern. All through Danny's illness she had been a tower of strength. She had made sure the kids hardly missed a day's school, visited Danny daily while he was in hospital, sometimes spending many hours there, before rushing home to see the kids and commencing the household chores. She confessed it was often turned twelve o'clock at night before she finished her work. Now Danny was home she became his full time nurse as well as mother of two and housewife of the year.

The last four months had been a nightmare for her and we had never seen her weaken or crack. Although the offers of help poured in from her family who lived in the area and ourselves, she would only accept it as a last resort, always trying to manage things by herself. But now Danny was at last on the mend, Sue began to show the first cracks in her emotional armour. We had all noticed the change in her. She had become distant and humourless. Her usually smart appearance had been replaced by an uncharacteristic disregard for the way she looked. Her lovely, dark. Chestnut hair had lost its sheen and her soft, brown eyes had no sparkle. She had held herself together for so long she had used up all of her energy. Now she was running on empty, her life force was reading nil and something had to be done.

Late April is birthday time for Marie, and I had been planning to take her to the sun for a surprise, but the more I saw Sue go downhill the more I thought that a change in plan might be in order. So one night I sat Marie down and told her what I had in mind.

"You want me and Sue to go away together?" she

said.' "It will do you both good. Sue is almost all in, and if she doesn't get a break soon God knows what will happen. And it will be a nice break for you, away from the kids and me," I told her." But it won't be the same without you and the kids.

I haven't had a girly holiday since I was eighteen and we all went to Skeggy for the weekend in a caravan."

"Well, now is your chance to make up for lost time," I told her. "And it was always going to be difficult for me to leave work, so it's best if you and Sue go together and just chill out for a week."

"What about the kids. You can't look after them while you're at work. And then there are Sue's kids,

Danny can't look after himself, never mind two kids," she protested. "It's all taken care of," I said. "Look, I've already run this past Danny. He says Sue's mum will take their kids for the week and my mum will take our two. So its' all sorted, and we both agree that it will do both of you the world of good."

"You've forgotten one thing," said Marie. "What's that?" I answered.

"Danny. Who's going to look after Danny? He can't even get out of the chair without help, or go to the toilet, or make a cup of tea. He would never survive a day never mind a week."

I tapped the side of my nose with my finger. "All taken care of," I said. "I'm going over to stay with Danny for the week. I can drive to work easy enough from Donni and I'll be there in the morning to help him out of bed and stuff, and then I'll be there every night to look after him. Sue's mum will check in on him in the day, so you can see it's all worked out."

Marie stood up and scratched the end of her nose, "Does Sue know about this?" she asked.

"Not yet, but I don't think she will say no, not in the state she's in. And if she does, we'll just tell her it's all arranged, so she has to go."

Marie walked over and wrapped her arms around me, "You're a good man," she said. "I'm glad I married you."

"Here, don't think I'm giving you carte blanche to shag all those good looking Spanish waiters, you know."

"The thought never crossed my mind," she laughed.

This had not been an easy decision for me. Marie and I had never been apart for more than a few days without seeing each other and I did not relish the idea of her being away for a week, but given the circumstances, it just seemed the right thing to do.

A week later, I stood in Manchester airport departure lounge waving Marie and Sue off. I had given her last minute instructions on staying together and avoiding dark and deserted places, and keeping Sue off the red wine etc., but I still wondered if I had made the right decision and the knot in my stomach wasn't helping much.

As I drove home, I castigated myself for not being more selfish and leaving Danny and Sue to sort themselves out. Deep down I knew that was just my own fears getting the better of me, and once at home I busied myself packing a suitcase for my stay at Danny's.

Marie rang that evening to say that they had arrived safely and were settling into the hotel. It was just after ten on a Saturday night when I arrived at Danny's, Marie's phone call had put me in a better frame of mind and I had brought a few cans of best Yorkshire bitter to share with Danny before crashing out for the night. Sue had given me a set of keys, so I could come and go without disturbing Danny.

I quietly turned the key and opened the door. Danny may well be asleep already, so I thought it best to creep in just in case.1 needn't have bothered Danny was laid out on the sofa surrounded by beer cans, half of them empty. There were also empty crisp packets strewn around the room, and the crumbled remains of a packet of chocolate digestives.

Danny gave me a chocolate grin, "Ah, Baz, my lad, I've been waiting for you. Do us a favour and make a sandwich. There's some cheese in the fridge, and don't forget to put a spot of salad cream on top."

"Right, salad cream," I said, as I headed for the kitchen.

"And put plenty of butter on the bread," shouted Danny.

"Right," I said.

"Oh, and could you make sure the butter goes right to the edges."

"No problem, right to the edges," I answered.

"Oh, Baz."

"Yes!"

"Could you cut the crusty bits off, they cut my lips."

"Consider it done," I said. I had a feeling that this was going to be a very long week.

The following day was Sunday and we had decided to have a day out, so I pulled the car up to the front gate. Danny had been given a crutch by the hospital but preferred to move around the house by grabbing hold of bits of furniture and hopping on his good leg. This was ok for a few feet but no good at all for a trip up the garden path. "You'll have to use your crutch," I told him.

"I can't get the hang of it," he said. "Anyway its slippery outside. I could fall and break my other leg. "Well, how are we going to get you to the car?" I said. "You'll have to carry me," Danny exclaimed. "You're joking. You weigh about fifteen stone and that's not counting your pot leg," I said.

"I know just the thing," said Danny. "There's a special way of doing it. I've seen it on the telly. You stand with your back to me, and I put my arms around your neck. Then you lean forward and lift me up. It's called the snail lift. You know it's like the shell on a snail's back."

"The snail lift," I said.

"That's what they call it," Danny replied.

"Ok, if you think it will work."

"Absolutely," Danny said. "It will be like lifting a feather so it will."

He had an air of confidence about him, but I had seen his confidence before. It usually came just before something blew up in his face. I backed up to Danny in the hallway and he clasped his hands around the front of my neck. "Hold tight," I said, and leaned forward until I was bent so far forward I was looking at my feet. 'Are you off the floor?" I croaked.

"That I am, Baz," said Danny. "Just look in the mirror." I glanced sideways at the long hallway mirror, to see Danny's legs sticking out vertically behind me. "We look ridiculous," I said. "We can't go out like this."

"Stop whining and start walking," shouted Danny. "We'll soon be at the car."

I began to move forward, one small step at a time. I couldn't lift my feet off the floor so I scraped along a few inches each step. Danny's hands were now gripping my throat and I was beginning to struggle for breath.

"The snail lift," I wheezed. "More like the big, fat Irishman lift." Shut up and keep moving. We're nearly halfway there."

At that moment a group of teenagers were passing the house and, seeing the sight of me bent double with a stiffened Irishman with a pot leg lying vertically along my back, decided to stop and see how it all worked out.

"Hey, mister. You've got something stuck to your back."

"Hey, quasi, one lump or two?"

"Are you two Siamese twins?"

"Just ignore them," Danny said." Well, I'm hardly going to chase them away with you welded to my back, am I?"

"Tch, tch aren't we cranky today? Just because you're not as strong as you thought."

As we reached the end of the garden path I felt a sudden twinge in my back, but I had to carry on for fear of dropping Danny. The lads were having a field day.

"Do you want us to throw a bucket of cold water over you mister? It works with dogs."

"Just do me a favour and open that car door will you, son," I said to one of the quieter of our tormentors. He opened the door and I turned and positioned myself so I could stand up. With Danny next to the passenger door, I stood up very slowly, the pain in my back was now intense, but it was a relief when Danny let go of my throat and I could breath freely again. Danny sat down and pushed the seat back as far as it would go then, gingerly lifted his pot leg into the car.

I limped around to the driver's side still clutching my injured back. As I eased myself into the driver's seat one of the teenagers shouted a final jibe, "Take my advice mister. Next time you be the giver, it won't hurt your back as much, ha ha ha."

Danny lowered his window and shouted, "It sounds as though you know what you're talking about young fella. I should watch him lads." As we drove off we could see the lad trying to explain to his mates how he knew so much about giving and receiving.

My back felt better now I was sat down and we decided to drive to Cleethorpes because Danny wanted a candy floss. He also had some fish and chips, an ice-cream, a plate of cockles, and a bag of those doughnuts that are made on the spot and dipped in sugar. Afterwards we drove down to Humberston, opposite Spurn Point and watched the big tankers and container ships sailing up and down the Humber. We came back along the coast road through Grimsby and Immingham where we stopped for a while to watch the ships unload at the massive docks.

It had been an enjoyable day out, just cruising and winding down with Danny. But as we turned south to Doncaster I began to feel the twinges in my back and by the time we hit the outskirts, it had become excruciatingly painful. As we pulled up outside Danny's house, I was in agony and had stiffened up so much I couldn't move.

"I don't think I can move, Danny," I said between the waves of pain.

"You've only pulled a muscle in your back, its nothing now come on and help me inside," said Danny impatiently.

"No, no, honestly mate, I can't move. I'm... Arrggg... stuck." The merest shift in position now caused me intense pain.

Danny was unsympathetic and sat with his arms folded across his chest. "Some bloody nurse you are," he exclaimed. "I'm the one who needs looking after and all you can do is whine about your back. "If it hadn't been for your silly bloody snail lift, I wouldn't be like this," I snapped.

"Oh that's right, blame it on me. Now it's all my fault. "Of course it's your fault. There's a perfectly good crutch in the house but do you learn to use it? No. You would rather break my spine instead." Danny sat tight lipped and huffed and puffed, as I tried desperately to think of what to do next. We must have looked complete idiots sitting in the car outside Danny's house in the dark. The neighbours must have wondered what we were doing.

Eventually Danny piped up, "Well, I suppose it's up to me then." I turned to look at him slowly. Even the smallest movement sent electrifying jolts of pain shooting across my back. It was so bad that after each bolt of pain I couldn't talk or even get my breath for a few seconds.

"It's... up to you... now," I gasped. "You'll have to go in... and... Arrghhh... call an... ambulance for me."

"What? If you think I'm having an ambulance wailing up the street just because of a little back strain, you've got another think coming," said Danny. "Now I'm going to hop in somehow and you'll have to follow me. I've never known anyone carry on so much because of a simple pulled muscle." With that Danny swung open the car door and lifted his pot leg out, followed by his good leg. He then pulled himself up, by grabbing the top of the open door with both hands and hoisting his body off the seat. After a few seconds rest, he propelled himself forward on his good leg with a succession of small hops. His pot leg was held out in front of him and, was going really well, until he got to the garden gate, which was closed. He had to stop and reach over to open the latch.

Having managed to open the gate, he had to find his momentum again. But he also had to hold the gate open because it was on a spring. So, with his good hand holding the gate and his gammy leg out in front like a figurehead on an old sailing ship, Danny set off again. He had just let go of the gate and was almost clear, when it sprang shut and clattered onto his good, hopping leg. Although he still kept hopping, the blow had knocked him off course and in an effort to remain up right he took giant hops through the flowerbed and onto the lawn. I hadn't seen the gate hit him so I had no idea why he was suddenly hopping crazily all over the front lawn.

"Stop showing off," I gasped through the open passenger door but to no avail. I watched, in disbelief, as still hopping, he disappeared round the side of the house.

"Where the bloody hell has he gone now?" I said to myself, as I sat there not daring to move. Suddenly I saw Danny come back around the house, still hopping crazily from side to side. He was shouting something but I couldn't quite make it out, until he came up to the flowerbeds again.

Then I heard him. "Oh shit, oh, shit, oh shit," he was shouting after every hop. He cleared the flowerbeds with a mighty hop and landed square on the garden path.

"Ooohhh shiiiiit." He was now only a couple of yards from the front door and a few hops and shits later, he was hanging on the doorknob puffing and panting.

'At last,' I thought. 'Now he can stop fooling around and go inside to call me an ambulance.' But he was still slumped up against the door, and seemed to be fiddling with the handle.

"What's wrong?" I gasped. "Why don't you go inside and call for help?"

Danny looked up slowly. I could see the beads of sweat on his face, glistening under the porch light and his white teeth, shining into a sickly grimace.

"I've left the keys in the glove box," he gasped. "I'm totally fucked. You'll have to bring them."

My heart sank. I now had no alternative than to put myself through intolerable pain, just because Danny had hopped off and forgotten to take the front door keys with him. I made a mental note to kill him, if I survived the next half hour. I slowly snaked my left hand over to the glove box, not daring to turn my head in case it brought on the searing pain. I dropped the glove box door and gingerly felt around, until my hand came across the keys. So far, so good, but now came the hard part. I had to somehow get out of the car, without ending up unconscious from the pain.

I opened the door with my right hand, still staring straight ahead. This was it. I took a slow deep breath and began to inch sideways. To my surprise the pain was not as bad as I thought. I now had my legs out of the car, but I still had to stand up. After another deep breath, I leaned well forward and, taking all the weight on my legs, I stood up. I felt a twinge of pain but nowhere near as painful as I thought it would be.

I was now gaining confidence as I closed the car door and shuffled on to the pavement and towards the garden gate. I must have looked like Frankenstein's monster as I walked stiff legged and straight backed, with my arms rigid by my side, not daring to look left or right and my face set into a kind of scowl. I shuffled up to the garden gate and tentatively pushed it back with my foot. I could see Danny looking at me hard, but I dare not speak or I would shatter my frail concentration and risk doing something silly, like turning my head or twisting my body and that would be catastrophic. Danny was still staring intently as I cleared the gate and began my arduous journey down the garden path.

Suddenly I felt a thump in my back. The gate had swung back and whacked me from behind. As I staggered forward, red hot flames of agony shot from my back. Some went down my legs, others down my arms and into my fingertips. I was struggling for breath as I dropped to my knees. Mist clouded my eyes as darkness engulfed my mind and I drifted into unconsciousness.

I must only have been out for a few seconds because the next thing I remember is Danny standing over me shouting, "Wake up, wake up."

"What happened?" I gasped.

"The gate hit you," answered Danny. "It did the same to me."

"Why didn't you warn me?" I groaned.

"I didn't want to put you off your stride. You seemed to be going really well," he answered. As I lay there on the garden path, racked with pain and looking up at the darkening sky, I remember two thoughts occupied my mind. One was how on earth was I going to get up again, and the other was how good it would feel to have my hands around Danny's neck and slowly choke the life out of him.

The front door keys had been retrieved from my clenched hand by Danny and he was now unlocking the door.

"Come on, Baz, we're in," he shouted. "You've only got to crawl another ten feet and your there. Or do you still want me to ring for an ambulance? I reckon you'd look a bit stupid laying there like a lemon."

"No ambulance," I wheezed. "I'll crawl." If it meant I could have the pleasure of strangling Danny with the telephone cable, I would have crawled a hundred feet."

"That's the spirit," said Danny. "Remember pain is all in the mind. Just don't think about it and it won't hurt."

"It doesn't hurt a bit," I kept repeating to myself, as I crawled along the garden path, up the front step and in to the hallway. Mercifully, my back seemed to have become numbed but my hands and knees were grazed and bleeding. As I reached the living room I just about had the energy to drag myself on to a chair.

Danny hobbled into the room and, seeing my disheveled state, exclaimed, "Fuck me, Baz. You look like shit. There's a crazy look on your face, and your eye is twitching. I'll make you a pot of tea and you'll soon feel better." I didn't have the strength to say or do anything other than groan, but as I drifted in to another bout of unconsciousness, I had this strangely satisfying image of Danny dangling from a telephone pole.

The rest of the evening was spent in a sort of nightmare world, filled with pain and strange images. Danny had dosed me up with some of his strong painkillers and I had foolishly taken them. Although the pain was tolerable now, I began to experience a strange, floating sensation and had difficulty telling dreams from reality. As the night wore on, Danny's pot leg seemed to treble in size and he began to speak in a different language. I would doze off and wake up to find myself in a weird place, where hands and feet were huge and heads were tiny. It was the longest and strangest night of my life.

I woke up the next morning with the world's worst headache and pain in my back that felt as though a thousand African fire ants had made their nest there. Not that I've ever been bitten by an African fire ant, or if there is such a thing, but if there were, and if a thousand of them had decided to burrow into my back and make a nest, then that's what it would have felt like.

Danny hobbled in with a mug of tea in his hand, spilling most of it as he wobbled over to me. "Ah, you've woken up then," he said.

"What did you give me last night?" I asked. "I feel like I've been run over by a bus."

"DF 118's, mate," he said. "The strongest painkillers known to man, except for a sledge hammer," he chuckled. "The doc told me to take one if my leg got to painful in the early days. It always took the pain off, but made me feel a bit woozy."

"How many did you give me?" I asked." Two and a half," he answered. "I was only going to give you two, but I thought oh what the fuck, in for a penny." You could have killed me."

"Nahhh, I think that's four or five," Danny said glibly.

I groaned and tried to sit up. It took a moment or so before I could prop myself into a position that caused me the least pain.

"See you couldn't have done that yesterday," said Danny. "Do you want another one?"

"No I do not. I'll stick to aspirin from now on," I said.

"Suit yourself," said Danny. "But you'll regret it when your back gets bad again."

"If it wasn't for your stupid slug lift I wouldn't be like this," I said.

"Snail lift. It's called a snail lift and can I help it if you got it all wrong and fucked your back up," answered Danny indignantly.

"Slug lift, snail lift, its all rubbish anyway. I have to go to work. It's Monday morning, I can't afford to miss a day." Marie and I had recently opened a small shoe shop and we would occasionally wholesale to other shops or market traders. We had made the break into our own business after I had left the steel industry about four years previously. It was long hours and took a lot of hard work but, it gave us a fair living and I enjoyed being my own boss. But as I lay glued to Danny's settee, my back rigid to deflect the pain, it was obvious that I was having a day off. We had made contingency plans for such an occasion in the shape of Marie's younger brother, Brian, who was nineteen and waiting to go to college. We had arranged for him to hold the fort for us when it had been planned to go away together, so he was able to stand in for me for a couple of days while I was laid up at Danny's. Marie and Sue rang home on Wednesday, by which time I was feeling better. It was good to hear her voice and it seems Sue was loving the chance to relax and recharge her batteries.

I was full of admiration for Sue. I had only lived with Danny for five days and he had already crippled me and given me a near fatal overdose of painkillers. I was not sure if I could survive another three days with the big Irishman. I saw no reason to tell Marie of my troubles and ruin her holiday, so I said all was well and I would be at the airport at the weekend to meet her and Sue.

As it turned out, I was back at work by Thursday and we got through the week without further mishaps, apart from Danny losing a wire coat hanger down his plaster cast while trying to scratch an itch. It took me two hours to hook it out, using an old bit of curtain cable.

Saturday came and we were at the airport. Danny had made the trip with me and had learned to use his crutch. Marie and Sue looked brown and healthy and it was a joy to see them. I had missed her more than I thought possible and had vowed never to be away from her for that long again.

Sue was like a new woman, or it would be more accurate to say like her old self. The holiday had been just what she needed and the sparkle had returned to her eyes. "How have you two managed?" asked Sue. "Any problems?"

Danny and I looked at each other, "None at all," we answered in unison. "But it's good to have you both back," I added.

"So, you've missed us then?" said Marie.

"You'll never know how much," I said as I took the cases and headed for the door.

Danny had two months left before the plaster came off his leg but he and Sue were determined to be the first couple to use Dunroamin. The place had stood empty for almost six months and had never seen any action. So on a bright, sparkling Sunday afternoon in June the four of us drove into the rear car park of Dunroamin. We carried with us three bottles of white wine and a bottle of champagne; we were going to christen it in style. Danny somehow dragged himself up the iron stairway and I unlocked the door. It smelt stale inside but we threw open all the windows and Marie squirted air freshener around the place while Sue washed some glasses.

When everyone was ready, I popped open the bottle of bubbly. As I was pouring the champagne into the glasses Danny began to speak. "I, err, would just like to say something, if it's ok with you two." Sue went to stand by his side. "It's so easy these days to pay lip service to being good friends, and most people will be your friends when times are good. But you find your true friends when times are bad, when it's not so easy, and Sue and I would just like to say we have found our true friends. And we would like to say thanks for being there for us when it would have been easier not to have been and thanks for, well, just being our friends." Danny raised his glass. "A toast to friends," he said.

"To friends," we all echoed. I hugged Sue, I hugged

Danny, we all hugged each other. There wasn't a dry eye between us. Danny was right; there was a bond between us. It had been forged not just because we had shared Danny and Sue's adversity, but because we knew without a shadow of a doubt that they would have done the same for us. The sex that afternoon was not only tremendous, it was special. Sue and I enjoyed climax after climax, and when Danny and I were spent, we watched Marie and Sue make love for an hour. As a warm, early summer breeze came through the open window I turned to Danny and said, "I have a confession to make Danny."

"And what would that be?" he asked.

"Well, you remember when I did my back in doing the snail lift, and I accused you of making it up because I said I had never heard of it."

"Yes," said Danny.

"Well, I had heard of it, because I saw it on telly too."

"Ahhh," said Danny. "So you were just having a go at me because you sprung your back."

"Afraid so, mate. Sorry about that."

"That's ok, Baz, because you know those two and a half DF 118 painkillers I gave you."

"Yes," I said.

"Well, I gave you three."

CHAPTER 14

Looking Back

I need at least eight hours sleep a night. If I don't manage it I'm sluggish, mentally slow and incapable of holding much of a conversation, or as Marie would say a grouch. Whilst she on the other hand seems to survive on five or six hours sleep per night quite happily, always waking bright eyed and bounding with energy. It's always been a huge annoyance to me, knowing that I have to spend an extra two or three hours in the land of nod just to maintain a level of energy equal to Marie's. She is also naturally fit and took to the work-outs in the gym with an enthusiasm that I found hard to match. Even on my good days I was always ready to head off to the showers a good fifteen minutes or so before Marie had finished her round of exercises.

Her birth sign is Taurus and she certainly displays all the traits of the stubborn bull. Once her mind is made up, no amount of bullying, cajoling or pleading will change it. I've often said she has the body of a woman and the mind of a man, but that stubbornness has been her salvation.

As a young girl she contracted nephritis, a serious

kidney disease. She was taken into hospital and became so ill that the doctors warned her parents that she was unlikely to survive. But against all expectations she pulled through. Her sheer will to survive brought her back from the brink of death. One nurse told her mother that she had never seen one so young (she was seven years old) fight so hard to live.

When we were married a consultant warned her not to have children, as it would be too great a strain on her damaged kidneys, but true to form she brushed aside all concerns and proceeded to have two healthy daughters over a three-year period. She was ill for years after this but again fought her way through. Throughout all this time I worked in the steel industry in Sheffield, a hard backbreaking job that I detested, and with two small children and a wife, who suffered severe recurring bouts of kidney illness, I seemed to spend all my waking hours either working or on hospital visits.

As the years went by Marie's condition gradually improved and we decided that we would try to branch out and run our own business. I was sick of the daily grind at the steel works and longed to be my own boss and test myself in the world of business.

Our entry into swinging coincided with us starting our own business, which was a footwear shop and small trade wholesaler, so changes in all departments of our life reverberated around us at that time.

I tell this potted history because it is relevant to our lives as swingers. We had already been married for nearly ten years before we contemplated wife swapping and had had our fair share of hardship and setbacks. Our relationship was sound, adversity had already forged a bond between us, quite apart from the love we felt for each other, so swinging was not some flippant decision we took one night when we were bored with the telly. It was more of a natural progression within our relationship, a logical next step, if we wanted to continue to explore our boundaries. We were a couple who had experienced the pain and the pleasures of life together and had begun to rebel against the expectations of a society that demands conformity as a way of acceptance.

Neither of our personalities could or would ever accept that confining doctrine, and we felt we had earned the right to push our own limits, and now, as I lay awake watching the early morning light filtering through the bedroom curtains, my mind went back over the last five years. I smiled and grimaced alternately as different memories filled my thoughts. I almost burst out laughing as I remembered the first time Farmer Giles and Ginger had walked through the door of that strange little North Yorkshire pub. And the image of Danny laughing hysterically as the Queen of Sheba was being taken from behind by Marmaduke the Afghan hound will remain with me forever. I grimaced at the way we had plucked thorns from Curly's emaciated body as we pulled him from the thorn bush, remembered the warm sensual naivety of our first meeting with Helen and Robert and the brutal way our naivety was torn from us by Kenny and June. I smiled as I remembered the grim satisfaction I felt when Marietta gave Kenny a taste of his own medicine in her Chelsea dungeon and the despair we felt when Danny lay close to death in the winter of 85.

I could still smell the heather and see the twinkling lights of the road winding along the valley floor the night

I had made love with Marie high on the Yorkshire moors. That was the night we had decided to give swinging one more try.

We had come so far since then, done so many incredible things and met so many wonderful people it all seemed like a dream. It was 7:30 in the morning and the sun had already sneaked strands of light into our quiet world. Marie was still asleep. For once I had woken before her but I could not get back to sleep. My head was too full of memories and questions. One of the sun's rays had crept onto the bed and had touched Marie's hair, highlighting a dark gold that I had not seen before. Her mouth was open slightly, showing her shining, white teeth. There was a soft flush to her cheeks and her slow, rhythmic breathing seemed to add calm to an already sublime moment.

As more memories flashed into my mind's eye. I clenched my teeth and winced. I could still feel the base of my spine crunching into the stairs, as June took her pleasures in there tower block apartment And the emptiness of the drive home afterwards and the worst moment of all when Marie and I clung to each other in the middle of a raging storm. It had all been about survival that night.

We knew when we decided to expand our boundaries that we would meet dangerous situations, and we had. But we had survived, and that owed as much to the fact that we had a grounding in meeting trouble together as a team, as it had with us both having personalities that screamed for adventure.

There had been subliminal moments along the way, times that rose above all our expectation. Marie and

Georgina licking each other in a sea of red velvet; myself and Georgina reaching into a new dimension of sexuality on the massage table; the look on Marie's face when she first held a whip in her hand; Danny raising a toast to friendship the night we christened Dunroamin.

We had also met some couples who would be lifelong friends, Robert and Helen, Charles and Georgina, and of course the closest of all, Danny and Sue.

What had we gained from the last five years? We had found a few answers and raised even more questions. We had grown as individuals and as a couple, and on a basic level; our sex life had expanded into a new universe. We had experienced things we had previously only read about in top shelf magazines. Had swinging been what we expected? Hell, no. We had found a world so far removed from our hum drum existence we could never have prepared for the roller coaster ride we found ourselves on. Our expectations had been totally overwhelmed by the sights and situations we encountered.

What had we accomplished? I asked myself that question a dozen times, as I lay watching the morning sun melt the night time shadows.

We were still together. I suppose that was an accomplishment, if you consider how we had put our relationship under the microscope and laid it open to the closest scrutiny. We had looked for the cracks and then tested them under the most extreme condition, imaginable and they had held, passed all the tests. Way beyond breaking point and now we could push on with the confidence that nothing or no one could hurt us. We had faced our demons and won.

Gone were jealousy, suspicion and frustration. In their place we had found confidence, contentment and fulfillment. What lay ahead, the unknown. We knew the scene was multi layered and we had only peeled away the first layer. Underneath was a new, exciting, and dangerous place.

Marie had still not had the chance to fully explore her dream of learning the arts of female domination. That quest alone would lead us down a new and terrifying path. And we had yet to learn that there are people out there who made Kenny and June look like Sunday-school teachers.

The last five years had, in effect, been our basic training and we would have to call on all our stamina and skills to face the next five.

Marie began to stretch and turned towards me. "How long have you been awake?" she said.

"Oh, about an hour," I said. "I've just been laying here thinking."

"About what?" she asked. I leaned over to kiss her on the forehead.

"About whether to get up or go back to sleep," I said.

"You'd better try for another hour or two," she said. "Or you'll be a grouch all day."

"Me, a grouch, never." She got up, put on her dressing gown and bent down to kiss me.

"I'll bring you a cup of tea up and the Sunday papers in a couple of hours," she said.

"I could get used to that," I whispered.

"Oh, in that case I won't bring you one," she said. "Can't have you getting spoiled."

I furrowed my brow. "What! I had just got used to the idea of a nice cup of tea when I wake up. You will still bring me one won't you?" Marie opened the bedroom door and went out, a second later she popped her head back round, she had a smile on her face.

"That's part of the fun," she said. "The not knowing." With that she was gone, I buried my head in the pillow, pulled the duvet up to my neck, smiled to myself, and drifted off to sleep

If you want to know what happens next, read

Swingers 2
Going all the way... again

Published by Matador
ISBN 978-1905886-654